It Must Be Magic

Chapter One

"Did I miss anything?" Breathless, Kerrie Stewart slipped into a seat between her friends, Allison Howard and Jill McCafferty and finished the rest of her tuna fish sandwich.

"You're just in time," Allison said. "Look, there's Mike! They've only auctioned off Russ Monteith and Cathy Hobbs so far. Hey, doesn't Mike look cute in that turban?"

Kerrie felt her stomach turn. As if she needed anyone to point out Mike Price to her! She'd recognize him anywhere—even wearing a turban that looked suspiciously like a gym towel.

The auction was the kickoff for Junior Genie Week at Glenwood High. It was an annual event that everyone in the junior class looked forward to as a chance to really let loose.

Popular and prominent juniors were invited to dress up in Arabian Nights costumes and were auctioned off to the highest bidders. The auction took place on Monday, and for the rest of the week the "genies" had to perform all sorts of hilarious tasks for their "masters."

Kerrie recalled the highlight of last year's Genie Week, when the entire school turned out to watch Todd Weathers run around the track in the rain wearing a yellow slicker and lacy, pink shower cap. At the end of the week, there was always a parade and then a Saturday night dance, the Arabian Nights Ball. The theme for this year's dance was "Den of the Forty Thieves." Wistfully, Kerrie wished she were going.

She looked at the stage, watching Mike clown around before his bidding began. He smiled at the appreciative catcalls and laughter. How she envied his ability to look so relaxed and natural in front of people! Kerrie always felt self-conscious and clumsy when people were watching her—maybe that was the reason she kept her nose buried in a book so much of the time.

My trouble is I'm just too average. Straight, shoulder-length brown hair, blue eyes, and freckles across a snub nose. I'm shy around people I don't know very well. Kerrie knew she could never hold center stage the way Mike could.

Along with the towel turban, Mike was wearing an old pair of sweat pants. Someone had sewn strips of shiny fabric down the sides to make them look "haremish." *Marcy Connaway, I'll bet.* Besides being one of the most popular girls at Glenwood, a pom-pom girl, *and* Mike's steady, Marcy was a real whiz in home ec.

The group of kids waiting their turns to go up on the auction block—a box with a big cardboard Aladdin's lamp glued to the front of it—were so outlandishly costumed that Kerrie had trouble recognizing some of them. She picked out Kelly Wiseman, a pert, dark-haired cheerleader for the Glenwood Wildcats, and Bob Lauren, a varsity football player, who was whispering something in Kelly's ear that made her laugh out loud. Chris Teall, class secretary, wore striped pajama pants gathered at the ankles with rubber bands. Big, gangly Skeeter Hollis, the class clown, was mugging it up next to Jaynie Cox, who looked bored and gorgeous, every blond hair in place.

Kerrie could hear people whispering all around her:

"If I had Chris Teall, I'd make him scrub my car with his toothbrush."

"I'd like to get Linda Jordan for a week. I'd make her do all my biology homework. I hear she's a genius in lab."

"Man, look at Mike Price. He'll do anything for a laugh!"

Onstage, Mike executed a perfect cartwheel. Loud hooting and the thunder of stamping feet echoed throughout the building. Jill leaned close to Kerrie in order to be heard.

"By the way, Ker, happy birthday." Jill's blue eyes sparkled, and a smile of unmistakable mischief dimpled her plump cheeks.

"What's with you guys?" Kerrie demanded. "My birthday's not for four more days, but you've been acting like a couple of secret agents for weeks. I hope you're not planning another surprise party like last year's. Wow, what a disaster!"

Allison flashed her a sheepish grin. "I guess it *was* pretty bad, wasn't it? Maybe it would've been all right, though, if I hadn't forgotten to call out for the pizza."

"Yeah," Jill said, "it was pretty embarrassing ending up at McDonald's like that. Guess the whole plan kind of backfired."

Allison smoothed her shiny, dark hair, her pixie features lighting up with excitement.

She was the craziest of the three friends—the one who dreamed up all the surprises and then pulled the other two along with her. She always said it was for their own good, that Kerrie needed "livening up" and that Jill needed "to get her head out of the clouds."

"This time you *won't* be disappointed," she assured Kerrie. "Promise, cross my heart. It's something you never would have guessed in a million years. We had to come up with something really terrific for your sixteenth birthday, didn't we?"

The old, familiar saying ran through Kerrie's head: "Sweet sixteen and never been kissed." Of course, that wasn't strictly true in her case. She'd been kissed before—exactly twice. The first time in the seventh grade by Tommy St. Clair, but that hardly counted since it was only a peck and since, as she later found out, his friends had dared him to do it. The second time was last summer at Searsville Lake. She and Ron Kemp had volunteered to go up the beach to get hot dogs and Cokes for everyone. Ron was a quiet, red-haired boy, the son of her parents' friends. Kerrie knew he liked her, but it caught her completely by surprise when he pulled her to him and kissed her as soon as they were behind some trees. For some reason, all she could remember about that kiss was the taste of Sea-and-Ski.

It wasn't a kiss that would go down in history, that was for sure. Nothing like that scene out of *Saturday Night Fever* when John Travolta kissed his girlfriend on the dance floor. That was the way she imagined it would be with Mike; though, of course, it was ridiculous to imagine such a thing, and she would die before admitting her daydream to anyone. Mike barely knew she existed. And even if, by some miracle, they went out on a date, what difference would it make? He would only find out how dull and serious she was, and probably he'd be bored stiff the whole evening.

Casey Wilcox, junior class president and genie auctioneer, banged his gavel against the podium and motioned Mike forward as the bidding continued. A hand shot up, and a loud male voice called, "One dollar! But that's only if Marcy comes with the deal!"

There was a wave of laughter, and Kerrie noticed with envy how sensational Marcy looked in filmy, lilac chiffon harem pants and satin halter top decorated with shimmering sequins. With her dark-lashed blue eyes, long blond hair, and beautiful figure, she came about as close as anyone could to the perfect genie ideal.

"I'll bet she stayed up all night sewing that outfit," whispered Jill in a voice laced with what-could-she-possibly-do-wrong sarcasm. "Doesn't she know this whole thing is supposed to be a gag?"

Before Kerrie could comment, someone shouted from the other side, "Two dollars!" Kerrie recognized her as Libby White, a harebrained type who was always being sent up to the office for talking too much in class. She had plenty of friends, but no steady boyfriend that Kerrie knew of. Did Libby have a crush on Mike, she wondered?

Someone else came up with "two-seventy-five," and before long the bidding had gone up to eight dollars. The record for last year was twelve, and that had gone for Cheryl DiMarco, who was later crowned queen at the Arabian Nights Ball. Kerrie frowned a little as she thought about the ball. Allison was going with her steady, Kevin Butler, and the fact that Jill hadn't been asked didn't really matter to her. She was going up to San Francisco with her family that night to attend a cousin's wedding on Sunday.

Mike was making the most of the spotlight, Kerrie noted with amusement. Halfway through the bidding, he began doing a little shuffle step across the stage, earning a scattering of applause. He bowed low, palms together and elbows stuck out, in true genie fashion. His turban was slightly askew, and a few chestnut curls corkscrewed out on one side.

The first time Kerrie had really noticed him was at the beginning of the year, when he was assigned the desk in front of hers in art class. Most of the time she could see only his back. And one day she found herself with a ridiculous longing to wind her fingers among the curls along the back of his neck. The thought had made her blush.

One of their first assignments was to do caricatures of each other. Mr. Mueller had paired them off according to the seating arrangement, so Kerrie had ended up with Mike.

"Hey, you're really good," Mike said admiringly when she showed him the finished sketch. "Do you practice a lot, or does talent just run in your family?"

"Actually, my father's an artist," Kerrie confessed shyly. "Or at least, he was—a long time ago before he married my mother. Now he sells insurance." His present profession sounded horribly dull to her, even though she knew her father enjoyed it. He had a real talent for working with people—a knack Kerrie often wished she'd inherited.

"Well, you ought to keep at it yourself," Mike said. "Maybe you could go to art school after you graduate."

This was a serious side he rarely displayed. He always seemed to be joking and clowning with his friends.

"I'm planning on going to a regular four-year college," Kerrie told him. "But I don't know what I want to major in. And I don't know where I'll apply yet. What about you?"

He shrugged, an impish grin hiding any real feelings he might have had on the subject. "I don't know. I doubt if I'll get into any college with my grades. My counselor, Mr. Clarke, calls it a 'terminal case of laziness.' You'd better not get too close," he teased, "it might be catching!"

Kerrie didn't let on about her own A average. At that moment, she only wanted to share Mike's casual attitude toward school—and life in general. Why couldn't she relax more—learn how to just have fun? She couldn't imagine Mike or any of his friends lying awake at night worrying about a test, the way she often did.

Almost sixteen, she really hadn't done much dating. She felt shy and awkward going to dances with her friends. When everyone else was having fun, Kerrie had to work hard to keep smiling and to pretend she was having a good time. She didn't have the knack for offhand banter or the kind of teasing thrown back and forth between girls and boys. "Just be yourself" was one of her mother's favorite pieces of advice. Could she help it that plain old Kerrie Stewart wasn't exactly the kind of person who set Glenwood High on fire?

Allison insisted she had a sense of humor, she just had to "let it out more." Kerrie wasn't so sure. How could a person be serious and funny at the same time? "Face it," she said to Allison one day, "either you have it or you don't. There are simply no in-betweens."

Her social life was as dull as she felt. Weeknights she spent studying or reading, sometimes watching TV. On Saturday she often rode her bike or went hiking up one of the mountain trails nearby; at night she would go see a movie with Jill or Allison, when Allison wasn't out with Kevin. Once in a while, Ron Kemp would call her up—they were just friends now—and they would go for pizza or play miniature golf.

Kerrie was certain Mike's social life was infinitely more exciting. He would have no trouble at all getting dates.

They hadn't really talked again since that day in art class, but Mike always said hi to her in class or gave a friendly wave when he saw her in the halls. Little by little Kerrie realized that her daydreams about Mike were turning into a serious crush.

Kerrie thought she must be daydreaming now as she watched Allison's hand shoot up into the air.

"Eight dollars and fifty cents!" her voice rang out over the auditorium.

Another bid followed, and to Kerrie's utter horror, Jill countered, "Nine dollars!"

"What do you think you're doing?" Kerrie hissed at them.

Jill gave her a sly look. "You'll see. . . ."

Before Kerrie could protest further, a hush had fallen over the crowd, and she could hear Casey chanting, "Nine dollars? Do I hear nine-fifty? Don't tell me you're going to let this gem of a genie slip through your fingers? Just imagine the laughs you'll get having him around. . . ." He waited for the noise to die down, then brought his gavel down with a crashing flourish, and announced, "Sold! To the girl in the fourth row for nine dollars!"

Mike gave a thumbs-up sign to the audience and then did a quick sprint offstage. Kerrie was so dumbfounded, she couldn't find her voice. It didn't make any sense at all!

What were Allison and Jill thinking of? They both had to know how she felt about Mike.

It wasn't until Allison turned to her and spoke that the whole thing really came into focus, suddenly making perfectly awful sense. "Happy birthday, Kerrie!" she piped enthusiastically. "Told you it was going to be a big surprise, didn't I? You never would have guessed, right?"

Kerrie forced a weak smile to cover up the feeling of panic that was welling up inside her. "Never in a million years."

Chapter Two

"Your wish is my command, fair lady!"

Mike accosted Kerrie as she was trying, unsuccessfully, to slip out of the auditorium in the first surge of the departing crowd. His eyes crinkled with amusement as he looked down at her, unaware of her cringing embarrassment. She prayed he wouldn't guess how she felt about him.

"Hey, Kerrie," he said, dropping the mock baritone, "you don't mind, do you? Your friends told me about it being a surprise for your birthday and all. I think it's a great idea, really neat—having your very own genie. They must think you're something to come up with an idea like this."

"Yeah," she mumbled, ducking her head to rearrange the suddenly awkward weight of her books. Before she could stop him, Mike had snatched them out of her arms, ignoring her protests.

"Might as well start being useful right now," he told her. "How would it look, you carrying your own books with your genie standing empty-handed beside you?"

"Thanks," Kerrie said, then added lamely, "They were pretty heavy."

They rounded the corner of the building and drifted out into the quadrangle that was the center of the classrooms and offices making up Glenwood High. Redwood benches were placed along a juniper hedge, which framed the concrete patio, where several groups of kids were already gathered in tight knots, discussing the auction. Mike led the way over to a vacant bench and motioned for Kerrie to sit down.

"There are still a few minutes before the bell. I thought we could, you know, go over any ideas you might have—see if you can come up with some really dirty jobs for me." He grinned engagingly.

She knew he was teasing her, but even if it was all in fun, she felt resentful toward Jill and Allison. What made them think Mike would like her just because he was stuck with her for the whole week? They were too different—she wasn't his type at all. Why, all anyone had to do was take a look at Marcy to see that! Somehow, knowing he was being such a good sport about the whole thing only made her feel worse.

"I don't know, Mike." She tried to think of something witty to say, but nothing like that came out. "I never expected anything like this. I guess I'll have to think about it."

"I bet if we put our heads together, we could come up with something crazy enough to win the prize for best stunt at Friday's parade."

She had forgotten about the Genie Parade, when the whole school turned out to watch the genies and masters perform their best routines in costume. There were prizes for the best costumes, as well as ones for the most original stunt, best teamwork, and best all-around couple.

"Maybe," she answered, but her doubts sounded in her voice. What could she—serious, straight-A Kerrie—possibly dream up that would be crazy enough to earn a prize?

"It's funny," Mike observed, as if echoing her thoughts, "but I never thought I'd end up with someone like you."

Kerrie flushed, needled by his honesty. "We don't have to go through with it, Mike. I-I'll just tell my friends I changed my mind. Maybe it wasn't such a such a good idea after all."

"Hey, wait a minute! That isn't what I meant. I guess, in my own dumb way, I was just trying to say you're the last person I would have thought needed a clown like me hanging around. You always seem so"—he groped for the right word—"capable. That's it. That's something I admire. Honest."

She couldn't tell from his expression whether or not he was just making it up to save her feelings. His clear sea-green eyes regarded her seriously for a change; Kerrie felt a strange tingling sensation at being so close to him. She wanted to tell him how she hated her "capable" image, how she longed to be more like him—easygoing and fun-loving—but, of course, she could never confide in him like that.

He cocked his head to one side with a look that was halfway between serious and teasing. "You know we could really make a good team. With your brains and my reputation"—he grinned a little self-consciously at the last part—"I know we can really come out on top this week."

Kerrie felt the first flutter of excitement. "You really think so?"

"Hey, I know it!"

She caught her lower lip between her teeth. "OK, Mike. I really will try to think of something. I promise."

"Terrific." He was so close, she could see the tiny splinters of gold in his green eyes. She felt a strange sensation in her chest, as if there were a string there and someone had plucked it. "I'm counting on you, Kerrie. Don't let us down." She liked the way he'd said "us" instead of "me." The invisible string in her chest gave another ping.

Just then, the bell rang. Mike stood up. He towered over her—a lean, muscled six feet. With his turban off, his hair stood out in crinkly, reddish-brown curls, glinting where the sun had lightened the ends. He'd changed into a pair of plain Levis and a faded T-shirt. They looked just right on him.

"What've you got next?" he asked.

"Trig. Over in Building C."

He made a face. "Ugh! Never made it past algebra myself. Guess I'd have to make it up in summer school if I wanted to go to college." He was still holding onto her books. "Come on, I'll walk you. I've got government down the hall."

They were heading into the noisy, jostling stream of students when Marcy Connaway appeared out of nowhere to link her arm through Mike's. She had changed, too, into snugly fitting designer jeans and a striking purple velour top cut to a deep V. She managed to direct the full brilliance of her smile at Mike while ignoring Kerrie completely.

"Do you believe that Jeff Crosse? He bid eleven dollars for me just so he could get me to go to the dance with him—that's what he told me. You should have seen his face when I told *him* I was going with you. As if I'd be seen at the dance with a nerd like him anyway!"

Mike flashed Kerrie a sheepish look but didn't withdraw his arm from Marcy's. "C'mon, Marcy. Jeff's not so bad."

"Easy for you to say," she quipped, tossing her blond hair. "You're not the one who's stuck with a nerd for a whole week!" Taking notice of Kerrie for the first time, she shot her a quick maybe-I'm-wrong look. Kerrie caught her meaning and blushed.

"I can take those from here, Mike," she stammered, retrieving the bundle of books. "I've got to run, or I'll be late."

Was she mistaken, or did he look relieved that she was going? At any rate, he didn't argue, only grinned good-naturedly and waved goodbye.

"See you tomorrow, Kerrie."

"Sure, see ya, Mike."

She had just enough time to dash to her classroom and slide into her seat like a runner rounding home plate.

Kerrie unfolded the piece of paper that had been passed to her from Allison, three desks away. The note was short and to the point—like Allison. "How did it go with you-know-who?" she had scrawled in her large, loopy handwriting.

Kerrie glanced over at her friend, who was sitting staring straight ahead with an innocent expression on her face. She caught Allison's attention with a faint smile and a shrug. Let her figure that out! While Mr. Brandon droned on in his nasal English accent, which had earned him the nickname of "The Duke," Kerrie stared out the window and let her mind wander. The lawn stretched invitingly outside, cool and green; the smell of grass, still wet from the sprinklers, drifted through the open windows. As usual, her daydreams sneaked up on her, and before she knew it she was painting imaginary pictures of herself whirling in Mike's arms at the dance, wearing a dress that floated in soft waves about her. The dance was a slow one, the lights dim. He was looking down at her with that serious expression he saved for important times—his arms tightened around her, and he brought his face closer—she knew he was going to kiss her. . . .

"Miss Stewart." Mr. Brandon's dry voice jarred her back to reality. "If I didn't know you better, I'd swear you were daydreaming. If you intend to repeat your excellent performance on Friday's test—the only perfect score in the class, I might add—I suggest you pay attention to what I'm saying."

A titter rippled through the room. Kerrie frowned and looked down at her desk top; she hated it when teachers announced grades in front of everyone. Didn't they realize that super-good grades could be just as damaging to reputations as bad ones? People had a way of categorizing a bright person, calling you "Brain" or "Know-It-All." In grade school, some of the kids had called her "Kerrie the Brain"— as if that were all there was to her, as if nothing else counted.

Allison caught up with her after class as she was heading for her locker. "Boy, Ker, old Duke really gave it to you today! I've never heard him talk like that to you before."

"So? I'm not always Miss Perfect, you know." Kerrie banged open her locker door with more force than necessary.

Allison arched her brows in surprise. "What's

gotten into you, anyway? I thought being in love was supposed to make a person happier, not the other way around."

"Who said anything about love? Just because I happen to think Mike Price is a nice guy—"

"*And* good-looking," her friend put in.

"OK," Kerrie admitted. "He is cute, but that doesn't mean I have to be in love with him, does it?" She flung her trig book in, grabbed an apple, left over from lunch the day before, and bit into it savagely.

"Look," she went on, "don't think I don't appreciate what you and Jill tried to do for me, but I don't know if this is such a good idea. I mean, suppose he starts thinking I'm throwing myself at him, or something? He's too nice a guy to say anything that would really hurt my feelings, so how do I know what he's really thinking about me?"

Allison gave her a blank look. "You know, Ker, for someone so smart, you can be awfully dense at times. Did it ever occur to you that a guy might be nice to you just because he wants to be?"

"Like Ron, you mean," she replied glumly.

They both had study hall in the library during fourth period, so they didn't hurry.

"Ron's a friend, that's different. Maybe Mike

is being nice to you because he's attracted to you."

"Oh, right. Why should he be attracted to me when he's got Marcy?"

"Marcy's flashy, all right. OK, so you're not the flashy type. What's wrong with the way you are? I happen to think you're pretty terrific."

Kerrie cracked a reluctant smile. "Thanks, Al. Anyway, I'm sorry I yelled at you."

One thing about Allison, Kerrie thought, she didn't suffer from an inferiority complex, so it was hard for her to know how other people felt when their egos were trampled on. It wasn't that Allison was so beautiful, either. Like Kerrie, she had her good points and her not-so-good points. It was just that she never worried too much about herself. In that way, she and Mike were alike.

If you accepted yourself without too much fuss, other people would accept you, too, Kerrie thought. It seemed simple when she considered it that way, but Kerrie knew how hard it was to work at something that didn't come naturally.

Kerrie came to an abrupt halt at the double doors of the library. "I don't feel much like studying right now," she announced. "How about cutting for the rest of the day?"

Allison shrugged. In her own words, she was a good, solid middle-of-the-road student, which translated, meant that she didn't worry too much so long as her grades didn't fall below a C.

"Fine with me," she said. "But I thought you had that Spanish quiz to study for." Spanish was Kerrie's weakest subject, which only meant she had to work twice as hard for an A.

"Oh, who cares about Spanish!" she declared with sudden recklessness. "Let's go get a Coke at the Stagestop."

But even as she said them, Kerrie knew how empty her words were. Cutting study hall only meant she'd have to stay up later than usual to finish preparing for the quiz.

The Stagestop was a tiny hole-in-the-wall luncheonette in the heart of Glenwood Hills, where Kerrie had lived most of her life. Across the street, framed by oak trees, was the Glenwood Market where her mother shopped; next door was a Rexall's, then an antique shop, a feed store, and a fashionable boutique, all of which showed the contrast between the old rural ways and the newer suburban ones. There were several housing developments nearby, but many of the families, like Kerrie's, owned enough acreage in the redwood-thick hills to keep the developments from spreading too far.

Kerrie sipped her Coke, watching as several other kids drifted in and sat down at the counter or one of the other booths. It appeared that she and Allison weren't the only ones skipping school.

Some of the girls in the next booth were discussing their plans for the dance. "My mom's making my dress," one girl was saying. "We went shopping last weekend and picked out the material. Wait till you see it! She made me pick out a simple pattern, though, since sewing isn't really her thing."

"You heard about Marcy's dress?" her companion asked. "She's not only making it herself, but designing it from scratch, too. Mrs. Klein, our home ec teacher, says she has a real talent for designing, and maybe she ought to think about making a career of it."

"What does Marcy say?"

"Oh, you know her. She never takes anything too seriously except maybe Mike Price . . ." The rest of the sentence was drowned out by the whirr of the milkshake machine, for which Kerrie was grateful. She'd heard enough.

By the time school let out, the place was

really crowded. Several people had even brought their genies. Greg Linville sauntered in, grinning as he led six-foot-four Mark Reese by a length of chain made out of construction paper, to which he'd attached a papier-mâché ball. A ripple of laughter greeted them as Mark whipped out a bandanna and dusted off a stool for Greg to perch on.

Kevin Butler, Allison's steady, came in and slid into the seat next to Allison. He was easily as tall as Mark Reese but couldn't have weighed half as much—which was a constant source for kidding from Allison. He did eat more than anyone she knew. Naturally he was on the basketball team, along with Mike. He wasn't considered really handsome, but Kerrie liked his looks: narrow face with warm brown eyes, a dazzling smile, and a shock of brown hair that hung over his forehead.

Kevin took a noisy slurp from Allison's Coke, then grabbed some french fries off her plate. "I hear you and Jill really pulled a good one on Kerrie," he said. "I was talking to Mike today during practice."

Allison raised an eyebrow, asking innocently, "Oh? What did Mike have to say?"

Kevin shrugged and stuffed another fry into his mouth, which Allison had once dubbed "The Black Hole." "Not much," he answered and turned to Kerrie. "I gather he thinks you'll be a good influence on him—you know, like maybe your smarts'll rub off on him somehow."

"Is that all?" Allison pressed.

"Yeah, pretty much. Except I told him I wouldn't get my hopes up if I was him. You've got a pretty good head on your shoulders, Kerrie. Mike happens to be a confirmed nut."

"Maybe Kerrie likes nuts," Allison shot back defensively, while Kerrie suddenly became absorbed in removing a straw from its wrapper.

"Oh, yeah?" Kevin slung an affectionate arm about Allison's shoulders. "That must come from hanging around you for so long." He grinned wickedly, dropping a kiss on the end of her upturned nose.

Suddenly, for no good reason at all, Kerrie felt like crying.

Chapter Three

"Kerrie!" her mother called from the back yard. "Would you please take the cookies out of the oven when the timer goes off?"

As if on cue, the oven timer pinged. Kerrie grabbed a pot holder off the sink, opened the oven, and slid out a tray of good-smelling cookies. Sesame seed, she noted. They were OK, but definitely not her favorite.

Her mom was the only mother she knew who baked things like sesame seed cookies and zucchini cakes instead of chocolate chip cookies and brownies. When she was younger, Kerrie was always too embarrassed to ask her mother to bake anything for school parties or bake sales. Now that health food was becoming more fashionable, it wasn't so bad. She pried up a warm cookie with the spatula and took a bite.

Mrs. Stewart came in through the kitchen door, pulling off gardening gloves caked with dirt. "Not too many now, Ker. It's almost time for dinner."

Absently Kerrie inquired, "What's for dinner?"

"I thought I'd warm up the rest of the squash casserole from last night. I picked some lettuce so we can have a nice fresh salad to go with it."

When they had first moved to this house, Kerrie was in the first grade, and there were flowers sprouting up everywhere in the backyard. Mrs. Stewart hadn't wasted any time, though, converting the flower beds into a more practical vegetable garden. She always said you couldn't trust the vegetables they sold in grocery stores, since you never knew how fresh they were or what kind of pesticides had been sprayed on them.

Kerrie knew she should be glad she'd been raised in a health-conscious family. She'd never had a weight problem, as Jill did, and people were always remarking about her clean complexion. "Wholesome" was the word people, like her parents' friends, used to describe her. It always made her feel funny, like a loaf of bread or something.

"Sounds good," she said, although she wouldn't have minded a double cheeseburger dripping with grease instead of the casserole.

"How'd it go at school today? You get your grade back on that trigonometry quiz yet?" Mrs. Stewart pushed a strand of straw-colored hair from her perspiring forehead. Her cheeks, in spite of their deep tan, were flushed from being out in the sun.

"Mmm-mm," mumbled Kerrie through a mouthful of cookie.

"Does that mean yes or no?" Mrs. Stewart asked. She carried a newspaper full of freshly uprooted lettuce over to the sink and began rinsing it off.

"I got an A," Kerrie announced matter-of-factly.

Her mother patted her arm with a damp hand. "Good girl! Your father and I are really proud of you, you know. I only wish Leslie would take her schoolwork as seriously. You're both bright, but you've always taken your responsibilities more to heart, I guess."

In Kerrie's opinion, fourteen-year-old Leslie was better off the way she was. Though this was only her freshman year at Glenwood, Leslie had really taken to high-school life. With her bubbly, outgoing personality, she was quick to make friends; and by the end of the first semester, she was on the Freshman Board and had signed up for membership in several clubs, including the Players' Guild. She'd even gotten a minor role in their production of *On Borrowed Time.* Kerrie could imagine Leslie easily charming someone like Mike, knowing just the right things to say.

"I'm thinking of dropping Spanish," Kerrie announced, surprising herself as much as her mother, since it was the first time it had entered her mind.

Mrs. Stewart looked about in dismay. "Why, Kerrie, I thought you were doing so well! I know you've had trouble with it, but look how much you've improved. Why would you want to give it up now?"

If her mother had just said "OK" or "it's your decision, dear," she probably would have let it drop right there. But for some reason, at this moment, her mother's attitude seemed to represent all that was wrong with her life.

"It's not as if I'll be living in Spain or Mexico after I graduate," she argued. "I honestly don't see the point in learning something just for the sake of getting an A on my report card. There's more to life than getting good grades, isn't there?"

"Of course there is! But an education is *so* important, honey. You'll never know how many times I wish I hadn't dropped out of college to marry your father."

"I'll bet you never tell Dad that."

"Oh, you know what I mean. I'm not sorry I married Dad, but there's no reason a girl can't get married and finish college at the same time. Of course, things are so different today, girls like you have so many more choices. . . ." Her sentence trailed off.

"That's just what I mean, Mom," Kerrie complained. "Why shouldn't I have a choice about dropping Spanish? Like you said, it's my life."

"Yes, it is, Kerrie," agreed Mrs. Stewart softly. "I just hope you know what you're doing with it."

"I can't stand it!" Leslie's blue eyes—carbon copies of their mother's—shone with excitement. "If I don't tell someone, I'm going to die!"

Leslie had tracked Kerrie down in her room as soon as she got home from school. Whatever she was dying to tell Kerrie obviously couldn't wait; she twirled around on the rug, scattering her books and papers in a kaleidoscopic pattern across Kerrie's bed.

31

"Hey, watch it—" Kerrie started to protest, but Leslie cut her off in mid-sentence.

"You're never ever going to guess what happened to me today—the most fantastic thing in the whole world!" She flopped down next to her books, rumpling the quilted spread. Her blond curls were fluffed up all over her head, reminding Kerrie of a baby chick's feathers.

"Well, tell me then. But if you're going to die, I'd rather you didn't do it on my bed."

Leslie popped up, facing her sister. She grinned, showing a mouthful of shiny braces, which hadn't kept her from smiling since the day they were put on. Kerrie remembered when she herself had worn braces in the seventh and eighth grades. For almost a whole year, she'd been afraid to open her mouth to speak.

"Robbie Markovich asked me to the Arabian Nights Ball!" she shouted. "Can you believe it? Isn't it fantastic? There's only one other girl in the freshman class besides me who got asked."

For a moment Kerrie felt resentful. But she knew Leslie wasn't showing off—and it *was* exciting, even if she wasn't in the mood to share it. Robbie Markovich was in Kerrie's

English class, and though she didn't know him well, he seemed nice. Kerrie remembered a poem he'd written and read aloud in class about his grandmother's funeral. She'd thought it was pretty brave to open up in front of everyone like that.

"That's really great, Les," she said, trying to sound enthusiastic. "I'm really happy for you. Have you told Mom and Dad yet?"

A tiny frown momentarily clouded her face. "Do you think they'll let me go, Kerrie? I know I'm not supposed to date until next year, but this is special. Besides, we'd be doubling with some other couples. Robbie has a VW van, and he's a really good driver."

"Hey," Kerrie said laughing, "you don't have to convince me. Dad's the only one you'll have to worry about—you know how strict he is about dating." *Not that he's had much of a reason to be with me,* she added silently. "I think if he met Robbie first, he'd come around."

"You think so?" She chewed a thumbnail, her one nervous habit dating back to thumb-sucking days. "Do you think you could talk to him, Kerrie? Please? You know Robbie, you could put in a good word for him."

Kerrie would have found it impossible to say no to her sister's pleading, even if she'd wanted to. She gave Leslie's hand a playful swat. "Yeah, sure. Why not?"

By the time dinner was over, it was all settled—on the condition that Mr. and Mrs. Stewart meet and approve of Robbie first. But, as Leslie knew, that would be no problem, and she was already planning what to wear and how she would fix her hair. She called half a dozen of her friends before Mrs. Stewart confiscated the phone for the evening.

When Kerrie was in her pajamas getting ready for bed, Leslie brought in a copy of *Seventeen* magazine to show her a hairstyle one of the models was wearing, glossy curls through which baby roses were woven.

"What do you think?" she demanded. "With the dress I wore at Aunt Celia's wedding?"

"Nice," replied Kerrie absently, pulling a brush through her hair until it crackled.

Leslie gave her a funny look, then closed the magazine. "I'm sorry, Ker, I guess I wasn't thinking—you know, about you not having a date yet and all." She stressed the word "yet" out of politeness.

"It's no big deal," Kerrie lied. "I don't really care if I go or not."

But Leslie wasn't fooled for an instant. "What about Ron? Why hasn't he asked you?"

"He's taking Sylvia Hendricks."

"Oh."

"Well, it's not like he's my boyfriend or anything. Sylvia's crazy about him—she told Jill so on the bus the other day." Briefly she wondered if Sylvia had ever dreamed about Ron the way she did about Mike. Then Kerrie replaced her brush on the tall maple dresser, turning her thoughts to more immediate worries. She'd promised Mike she would think up a genie stunt for tomorrow; he was counting on her. But what? For once in her life, her brain seemed stuck. Or was it just some kind of mental block against becoming too deeply involved? Was she afraid of getting hurt or making a fool of herself—or both?

Leslie wasn't much help when Kerrie asked if she had any ideas. "Why don't you make him carry your books around, or something?"

"Now that's what I call really imaginative." She gave her sister a scornful look. "Besides . . . he already carried my books."

"Oh?" Leslie arched her eyebrows. "I'll bet Mike's a real knight-in-shining-armor under that clown act."

"Oh, sure!" Kerrie giggled at the image of Mike charging down the halls on a white steed, armor clanking.

But the notion of knights touched off an idea. She was suddenly reminded of a pair of costumes her mom and dad had made for a Halloween party a few years before. As far as she knew, they were still at the back of their closet. Kerrie went to find out.

She returned a few minutes later with a shopping bag, which she dumped onto her bed. Her dad had made his mask out of papier-mâché, and although it was now a little faded, the artistry shone through: it was a unicorn head, with beautiful slanting eyes and a spiraling horn painted shiny gold. Her mother, who was an expert seamstress, had fashioned a medieval-style gown out of yards of gauzy material, even putting together a pointed cap out of cardboard and covering it with gold foil wrapping paper. Kerrie tried on the cap, then went to examine her reflection in the mirror.

Leslie looked at her as if she were crazy. "What do you want with those old things?"

"I'm not sure," Kerrie answered.

They were terrific costumes. The idea was for the unicorn to be led around by a scarlet ribbon that threaded through a gold ring stuck in his nose. But did she have the nerve to go through with it? And what would Mike think of the idea? In the end, she decided she wouldn't make up her mind until she'd talked to him and shown him the costumes; she'd bring them to school and see.

Kerrie knew she wasn't going to sleep a wink that night.

Chapter Four

Kerrie was making her way through the halls to her first class, US history, when a bicycle bell dinged for her to clear the way. She skipped aside just as a red wagon barreled past, giving her a glimpse of Dave Palmer, bell in hand, being pulled along by Linda Jordan, wearing a pair of paper donkey ears. They were followed by whistles and shrieks of laughter.

Junior Genie Week was in full swing.

Jill, munching on a doughnut, was waiting for her when she got to her locker. "I tried calling you last night," she said, "but the phone was busy for ages. You wouldn't, by any chance, have been talking to—"

Kerrie cut her off before she could go any further. "Blame it on Leslie. She was telling the whole world about her date for the dance with Robbie Markovich. I think she was just calling the White House when Mom took the phone away."

"Wow, how did she ever get so lucky?" Jill's round face mirrored a touch of envy. "Robbie's a great guy—how come the great guys are all taken?"

"No taste, I guess."

"Ve-ery funny, Ker. With your sense of humor, you should be able to knock Mike dead." She finished her doughnut and wiped a sprinkling of powdered sugar from her chin. "Speaking of the devil, I haven't seen him around this morning. Aren't you supposed to meet him or something?"

Kerrie stuffed the shopping bag containing the costumes into her locker, hoping Jill wouldn't ask what was in it. "I don't know," she replied evasively. "I forgot to ask."

"After all the trouble Allison and I went to? You've got to be absolutely crazy, Kerrie! If you don't start getting more involved in this thing, he's going to think you don't care. In more ways than one," she added, lowering her voice to a dramatic whisper.

"What's the difference?" Kerrie banged her locker shut and twirled the combination. "He's

Marcy Connaway's boyfriend, in case you haven't noticed."

"Since when do you give up so easy? I'll bet if Mike was a homework assignment, you'd have him eating out of your hand by the end of the week."

"That's just the trouble. He hates school-work—so what do we have in common?"

Jill's expressive blue eyes twinkled. "You've heard the old saying about opposites attract-ing, haven't you?"

"In this case, I'm not so sure it applies. Even so, how would you suggest I go about attracting someone like Mike?"

Jill giggled. "Well, you're not exactly asking the world's expert, but I think I've read enough books to take a guess."

Jill, Kerrie knew, was a voracious reader of romance novels. She claimed it was good train-ing for when she met her own "dream man." Kerrie thought again how different she, Jill, and Allison were, and wondered how they managed to stay such good friends.

"Allison says I should just be myself," Kerrie told her.

"Forget that."

"Thanks a lot!"

"No . . . that's not what I meant. There's absolutely nothing wrong with *you*. Maybe

all you need is just to loosen up a little bit
around Mike—you know, laugh at his jokes
and stuff like that. Show him you have a
sense of humor, too. Have you thought up
any really good genie ideas yet?"

"Not yet," Kerrie lied. Last night's brain-
storm had given way to a fresh crop of doubts
by morning; she hadn't even seen Mike yet,
and already her courage was seeping away.

Jill rolled her eyes. "What are you waiting
for—someone to wave a magic wand or something?"

Now that wouldn't be a bad idea, Kerrie
mused.

"Seriously, Kerrie," Jill went on, "even I
know that if you like a guy you've got to give
him half a chance to like you back. Look
what happened to Scarlett O'Hara!"

"Oh, great, now you're comparing me to
Scarlett O'Hara!"

"Well, at least she had the right idea in the
beginning. She knew how to flirt. It was just
too bad she didn't see Rhett for what he was
until the end."

Kerrie groaned. "What do I know about flirt-
ing?" She hated the way some girls made
absolute fools of themselves when they liked
a guy. They were so obvious! And yet, she

had to admit, it certainly seemed to work for some people—Marcy, for instance.

"I'll think about it," she told Jill.

"You'd better." Jill raised a threatening fist at her friend, then her expression turned dreamy. "Just think, if Mike asks you out, you could write your own romance."

Fat chance! thought Kerrie. She'd be lucky if she ever got past page one.

Their classes were in opposite directions, so they parted at the drinking fountain by the quad. Kerrie noticed with amusement that Kelly Wiseman's master had put her to work turning the handle for anyone who wanted a drink of water. A handmade sign taped to her back read: "You turn me on!" As a result, there were at least thirty kids with sudden cases of raging thirst lined up waiting their turns.

Kelly, of course, took it all in stride and was having a great time squirting all the kids in the face when they least expected it. Kerrie couldn't help wondering, as she hurried past, how *she* would feel in the same situation. Well, it would be one way of breaking the ice, she thought.

Maybe this genie thing wasn't such a bad idea. After all, what other chance would she ever have to see Mike and show him there was more to her than just a brain? Allison was right—she ought to quit putting herself down. Even Jill had a point about trying to loosen up more.

Kerrie was so absorbed in her thoughts as she rounded the auditorium that she nearly ran into a lanky form wearing a Glenwood Wildcats sweatshirt.

"Excuse me." She looked up into a pair of brilliant green eyes. "Mike! I'm sorry, I just didn't see you. Guess I was thinking of hurrying to class to get there on time."

He fell into step with her, and she couldn't help noticing his easy stride and the way he made her feel important, just by walking next to her.

"Good thing I saw you," he said. "I was looking for you. Where've you been? I thought *I* was the one who was supposed to be hiding out in a bottle."

She laughed, thinking how much more at ease she felt. "I got here a little early this morning, so I went to the library to catch up on some homework I didn't get around to last night."

"Oh, yeah?" He grinned. "Wish I'd known where to find you, you could have helped me with mine while you were at it."

She couldn't think of anything clever to

say, so she simply told him, "Honestly, Mike, if you ever need any help I wouldn't mind."

"Really? I just might take you up on that sometime. Not this week, though. What kind of genie would I be if I let you go around doing things for me?"

He waved to Joe Ratliff, who was busy scrubbing out someone's locker with a toothbrush. "Hey, Rat, say hi to the tooth fairy for me, will ya?" he called out, ducking as the soapy toothbrush came flying through the air, missing his head by inches.

Mike turned to Kerrie. "Just don't ask me to clean your locker with my toothbrush, and we can stay friends, OK?"

Kerrie warmed at the word "friends." Did he really consider her a friend? "Nothing that drastic," she promised, smiling.

"I'm waiting to hear what you've got cooked up for me, though. At least give me a hint so I can prepare myself."

"Well, I—"

They were interrupted by the ding of a bicycle bell, and a pair of limply waving donkey ears once again announced the Dave Palmer-Linda Jordan express. Mike roared in laughter.

"Did you see those two? If that doesn't take the prize at the parade, I don't know what will!"

Blushing, Kerrie looked up at him. "Well, you never know."

"Hey, that gives me an idea," Mike said. "I don't have a wagon, but will a handy pair of shoulders do?"

"I don't get it," Kerrie stammered.

He seized her books and hunkered down. "Climb aboard and I'll show you how to ride to class in style."

"Oh, Mike," she started to protest, "I don't know if I can. I . . . ." Then she remembered her new resolution to show him she had a sense of humor, too, and managed to swallow her embarrassment, "Oh well, what have I got to lose?"

"Nothing"—he grinned wickedly at her as she hooked a leg over one of his shoulders—"except maybe your reputation."

Did being a genie qualify him to be a mind reader as well? Kerrie wondered, feeling a rush of reckless exhilaration as he lifted her into the air. She gave a tiny squeal as he sped forward, shouting, "Clear the way, everybody, we're coming through!"

People darted out of their path, then stopped to point and laugh, but for once in her life Kerrie didn't mind being in the spotlight. She was with Mike, and suddenly it seemed as if nothing bad could touch her. She thought of Jill's magic wand and suppressed a giggle. Well, if Kerrie Stewart could ride to class on Mike Price's shoulders, *anything* was possible!

"Hang on!" Mike called up to her as they rounded a corner and came upon a low juniper hedge bordering Building A, where her history class was. She yelled out loud and clutched his forehead as he cleared the hedge with a long-legged bound.

Kerrie caught a glimpse of an upturned face, which she recognized as Laura Patterson's, a girl who hung out with Marcy. Laura's expression of open-mouthed disapproval managed to stay with Kerrie until Mike skidded to a stop in front of her classroom.

"Maybe you'd better put me down here, Mike," Kerrie suggested, laughing breathlessly. "Mrs. Johannsen might not—"

"Not on your life, kiddo! I wouldn't miss the look on old Johannsen's face for anything!"

With that, he ducked inside, Kerrie's head just clearing the door frame. A burst of surprised laughter greeted them, and Mrs. Johannsen gaped in astonishment.

"Way to go, Kerrie," called Peter Davenport, a boy who'd never spoken to her before.

Kerrie's cheeks flamed red, but she couldn't stop grinning.

"You sure know how to get the upper hand

with a guy!" cheered Sondra LeBlanc, her wrists rattling with colored plastic bracelets as she applauded Kerrie.

Even Mrs. Johannsen couldn't keep from cracking a tiny smile. "Well, Miss Stewart, I'm sure this is your idea of a joke, but it may be just the thing to introduce the chapter we'll be studying today—'Slavery in America.'"

Everyone in the classroom cracked up, since it was the first time Mrs. Johannsen had ever shown them that she had a sense of humor. Which just went to show, Kerrie decided, you never knew about people.

Mike let her down at her desk with an easy flourish. Clearly, he was accustomed to getting so much attention. He winked conspiratorially at Kerrie, causing a quick hammering of her pulse.

"Th-thanks, Mike," she managed, scooping up her books. "That was quite a ride."

"Anything for you," he replied, giving her a brilliant smile.

It was just the sort of thing any genie might have said, but she found herself hugging it close to her throughout Mrs. Johannsen's droning lecture on the Civil War.

Crazily, she *was* starting to believe in magic. At least in the magic possibility that Mike might really like her.

*　　*　　*

"What in the world—?" Mike held up the unicorn mask, turning it over in admiring disbelief.

After that morning's crazy episode, Kerrie had finally worked up the courage to present Mike with her idea. She had run to her locker, grabbed the costumes and taken them to art class. Standing in the back of the room, she quickly outlined her plan before class started.

Mike slipped the mask over his head and gave a horselike whinny. He looked so funny—with the painted horsey leer and gaudy horn sprouting from his forehead—that Kerrie had to stifle a burst of laughter by clapping a hand over her mouth. When he took off the mask, he was grinning.

"Well, what are you waiting for?" he demanded. "Climb into that costume of yours, and let's knock 'em dead!" He pushed her into the art supply closet so that she could change.

Kerrie didn't argue, hastily pulling the gown over her jeans and blouse and nearly smothering under all the yards of frothy material. She settled the cone-shaped hat on her head.

"I feel like an upside-down ice-cream cone,"

she said apprehensively as she emerged from the closet.

Mike gazed at her for a long moment, as if seeing her for the first time. "You look exactly like a fairy-tale princess." Then his mischievous grin was back. "They're not going to believe *this*!"

By this time class had begun. Mike put on the mask again, then handed her the bright red ribbon. Kerrie blushed a dozen shades of red as they swept toward the front of the room, Mike snorting and prancing about, weaving his way between desks as he pulled *her* along by the ribbon, rather than the other way around. Order fell apart at once, and the class was reduced to instant hysteria.

Kerrie could hardly believe what she was doing. And yet—at that moment, it seemed entirely natural. No one was laughing at her, as she'd feared; they were all laughing *with* her and Mike. It was going to be all right. She could feel it. And the feeling sent a glow flooding through her. She discovered, with a tiny shock of surprise, that she was actually enjoying all the attention!

Suddenly Mr. Mueller, a gray-haired teacher known to be very spontaneous, yelled for everyone to grab their sketch pads and pencils and follow "the lady and the unicorn" out to the quad.

Soon Mike and Kerrie were heading a carefree procession that snaked its way through the corridors in the direction of the quadrangle. Jackie Short, who always carried her flute with her, had assembled her instrument and was piping away at an airy tune that had everyone whirling and skipping. Heads turned in disbelief as they passed the open windows of other classrooms along the way. Their mood was infectious, attracting catcalls and loud whistles all the way.

Kelly Wiseman caught up with Kerrie, murmuring, "You look absolutely fantastic. Keep this up and you'll have every genie turning green by Friday!"

A boy Kerrie didn't recognize stuck his head out the window of the chemistry lab and let out a long whistle as she passed. She surprised herself even more by pausing to wave and blow him a kiss.

"Hey, don't get *too* carried away with this thing," Mike teased, nudging her with his elbow. In reply, she gave the ribbon a tug, prompting him to yell, "Ouch!" He rubbed his snout as if it hurt.

Out on the quad, Mr. Mueller positioned Mike and Kerrie on a bench so the others could sketch them "in all their glory," as he put it. Kerrie was smiling so hard that by the end of the period, she felt as if the muscles in her face were about to crack.

When the bell rang, people from other classes clustered around them, complimenting Kerrie's dress and wanting to try on Mike's mask.

"Any minute now they're gonna start asking for our autographs," whispered Mike in her ear.

"Does that mean we're a hit?" she asked, smiling.

His eyes held hers for a moment. "You bet."

Chapter Five

"Got anything for a starving genie?"

Unannounced, Mike swooped down on the table where Kerrie, Allison, and Jill were clustered at lunch.

Kerrie stopped in mid-sentence. She'd been in the midst of regaling her friends with tales of the morning's wild escapades—most of which they'd already heard from half a dozen other sources. Word of anything unusual traveled fast at Glenwood. People had been coming up to her all morning, congratulating her on the costumes, wanting to know if she had any other "brilliant ideas." Lynn McBride had even invited her to eat lunch with her gang. Would wonders never cease? She had always thought Lynn and her friends were so stuckup. Maybe she'd allowed herself to get just as hung up on prejudices as everyone else.

Mike made himself right at home, squeezing in between Kerrie and Allison. "Would you believe it? I was in such a hurry to get to school this morning, I forgot to make a lunch."

Jill looked up from her bologna sandwich. "You make your own lunches? Does your mom work or something?" Kerrie could just see the pages in her mind filling up with information about Mike.

"Yeah," he answered, "she didn't use to, but since she and my dad split up, she needs the money. It's OK, but she has to work these crazy hours—she bought this print shop and the equipment's all pretty old. Every time she turns around something's breaking down."

"That's too bad," Kerrie sympathized.

He shrugged. "We make out all right. When school lets out I'll be working in the shop for the summer. Hey, with my grades, I've got to learn a trade as soon as possible. No college in its right mind would take me."

"You never know," Kerrie put in. "There's still a year and a half left before we graduate. I'll bet if you really worked on them, you could bring your grades up to college level by then."

"Think so?" He was looking at her with

real interest now. Was it her "brainy" reputation that had captured his attention—or something else?

Jill was kicking her under the table to get her to change the subject—to something more amusing, no doubt—but Kerrie kept on talking.

"I'm sure you're smart enough, Mike. With most people, it's just that they get into bad study habits in grammar school, and by the time they hit high school, it's too late." She smiled. "Well, almost too late."

"You mean I'm not an entirely hopeless case?"

"Not unless you think so." She could feel Allison's eyes on her and added, "It's all in how you think of yourself. You've got to have confidence."

"Wow . . . take it from the expert. Maybe you could give me a few tips sometime when you're not too busy."

"Anytime," Kerrie responded casually, in spite of the fact that her heart was pounding. She could tell from the look on Allison's face that she had passed the test with flying colors.

"Half my trouble trying to concentrate on homework is my kid brother," Mike said. "I sort of have to keep an eye on him when

Mom's not around. Talk about a one-boy demolition squad! At the moment he thinks he's Luke Skywalker, and he's always knocking over the furniture pretending he's fighting off hordes of storm troopers."

"Sounds charming," Allison muttered.

Mike chuckled. "He's all right—a little strange, but look who's talking. Can't blame him if he's got me to take after."

"Kids can sure be a pain!" Jill added. She had three younger brothers and a sister and was constantly complaining that she couldn't even go to the bathroom without tripping over someone or his or her toys.

Kerrie was enjoying this chance to get to know Mike while surrounded by the safe company of her friends. Talking to him seemed so easy and natural. She didn't feel very awkward around him anymore—maybe because she was seeing that there was a lot more to him than just his clowning around. He obviously didn't have it so easy at home, even if he pretended not to mind. Kerrie knew a lot of kids whose parents had gotten divorced, and they all suffered in some way or other. She was beginning to suspect that Mike's clowning was just a cover-up for deeper feelings.

"Would you like half of my sandwich?" she offered shyly. "My mother always gives me way more than I can eat."

Mike wasn't shy accepting. "Hey, this is really good!" he commented after he'd taken a bite. "What kind is it?"

Kerrie recalled with a twinge how apologetic she'd always been about her mother's cooking.

"Avocado and alfalfa sprouts," she said. "I think there's some cheese in there, too."

"Great stuff," he said, attacking the rest of the sandwich. "Sure beats the greasy hamburgers I've been picking up at the Stagestop for dinner. Even Kurt won't touch them, and believe me, he'll eat anything—even frozen pizza, and I mean *frozen*."

Allison made a face. "Ugh!"

"You ought to come to my house for dinner some night," Kerrie found herself saying.

Allison's eyebrows shot up, and Jill nearly choked on her corn chips. Kerrie could have killed them both.

Mike's face brightened. "Hey, that'd be great, I'd like that. Sure your mom wouldn't mind?"

"I'll ask her," Kerrie said, "but I'm sure it's OK."

What have you done? a tiny voice inside her was demanding. Plenty of girls she knew thought nothing of calling up guys to ask them out, but Kerrie never would have thought she'd have the courage. She was the traditional type who wanted the boy to ask her out first—or at least, that's what she'd always thought. Suddenly she didn't know what "type" she was anymore.

"Mrs. Stewart's a terrific cook," Jill put in helpfully, although Kerrie knew she was just being polite. She was a confirmed junk food addict. She was always going on diets, but they never lasted very long. "She has this fabulous garden and grows practically everything they eat."

Mike patted his stomach, announcing, "I'm convinced! What time's dinner?"

They all laughed.

There was a sudden commotion at the other end of the cafeteria, and everyone turned to look. Melinda Wasserman's genie, petite, dark-haired Cathy Dominguez, was busy setting up one of the tables with a checkered tablecloth, china, and silverware—even adding a vase with a rose in it. When Melinda was seated, she began serving fried chicken and potato salad out of a picnic basket. Each time Melinda would take a dainty bite from her drumstick, Cathy would wipe her chin with a big napkin. Both were trying hard to keep straight faces—and only barely succeeded. The rest of the cafeteria was in an uproar.

Mike whistled. "Now that's what I call service. Why didn't I come up with something like that? Instead, here I am, eating *your* lunch."

"Really, Mike, I don't mind," Kerrie protested. Actually, she couldn't imagine having him wait on her like that—even as a gag.

"Well, the least you can let me do is share my lunch with you tomorrow," he said. "I make a pretty mean pastrami on french bread, if I say so myself."

"Sounds good," Kerrie replied, but she wouldn't have cared if it were peanut butter and jelly, as long as he invited her to eat with him.

Jill nudged Kerrie with her elbow, whispering under her breath, "Uh-oh, trouble on the horizon."

She looked up just in time to see Marcy glide over from the cafeteria line, balancing a full tray. She looked even more stunning than usual, Kerrie thought with a stab of envy. Her blond hair was twisted in a french knot with soft, curling wisps trailing at her neck. She was wearing cream-colored slacks and a short-sleeved, pale pink blouse. Kerrie felt plain in comparison, even though she'd taken extra care with her appearance this morning, putting on eye makeup and choosing a maroon tucked blouse instead of a T-shirt to go with her jeans.

"*There* you are, Mike!" she cooed, dismissing Kerrie and her friends with a quick glance. "I looked everywhere for you, but, of course, I should have known you'd be off on one of your genie errands."

"Hi, Marcy." He looked uncomfortable but was quick to explain, "I figured you'd be pretty tied up with Jeff today."

She rolled her eyes. "That's putting it mildly! I know I'm supposed to be his genie, but all he wants to do is follow me around and talk." She giggled. "Pretty soon, people are going to start thinking we're going steady."

"Poor Jeff, he must really be desperate," Jill hissed in Kerrie's ear.

"You should be flattered," Mike told her. "Jeff's a nice guy."

"Definitely not your type, though," Allison muttered—which Marcy either didn't hear or chose to ignore.

"You're on his side? I thought you'd be jealous, Mike. After last night . . ."

"Marcy, c'mon, I don't think this is the time." He darted an embarrassed look at Kerrie, making her suddenly wish the floor would open up and swallow her.

"Oh, sorry, I didn't mean to ignore your friends." She flashed them a bright smile, which was about as sincere as an ad for toothpaste, Kerrie thought. "It's just that I *was* hoping we could be alone. I did tell Jeff I was eating with you. Why do you think I got all this extra stuff? You don't think I'm going to eat it all myself! I've got to lose ten pounds, even if this diet kills me!"

"You don't need to lose weight, Marcy," Mike assured her. His glance took in her petite, perfectly proportioned figure, as she had intended. "You look great."

How could anyone be so obvious! And Mike didn't even seem to notice how hard she was fishing for compliments!

"Well?" Marcy eyed him impatiently.

He got up with a quick nod to Kerrie. "Guess I'll see you later," he said. "Thanks for the sandwich."

Kerrie was nearly in tears as she watched Mike's bright orange sweatshirt retreating through the crowd. At one point she saw him put a hand on Marcy's shoulder to guide her around a table. A lump rose in her throat, which only got worse when she tried to swallow.

"Ooh—I'd like to strangle that Marcy Connaway!" cried Jill.

Allison snorted. "I think poison would be the right thing for her."

Finally Kerrie found her voice. "It's not Marcy's fault if Mike likes her," she said softly. "I mean—just because he's being so nice to me, doesn't mean anything's changed between them."

Allison lobbed a crumpled sandwich bag into the nearest trash can, then turned to glare at Kerrie. "With that attitude you'll never get anywhere with him!"

"Can't you see?" Kerrie slumped down, staring at the remains of her lunch. The morning's magic seemed as far removed as a dream she might have had the night before. "It's hopeless."

Jill crunched down on a corn chip. "Nothing's hopeless, Ker, you even said so to Mike a few minutes ago."

"That was entirely different."

"No, it wasn't. Remember when we were talking about Scarlett O'Hara? Well, even *she* didn't think it was hopeless when Rhett walked out on her in the end."

"She's right," Allison joined in. "Mike's interested in you; it doesn't take a genius to figure that out. So what if he's dating Marcy? It
doesn't mean she owns him."

Jill smiled. "Look at it this way. If Marcy
was a nice person, you might feel guilty taking Mike away. As it is, you're doing him a
favor."

Kerrie groaned. "Come on, you guys, be
serious!" How was it that even in the worst
situations, they could find something to laugh
at?

Well, *she* wasn't laughing.

Kerrie had worked her way through one
pencil eraser and was chewing her way through
another when Mr. Garcia called for them to
hand in their test papers. Now she was sorry
she hadn't studied harder for the quiz. She
had a sinking feeling it was going to be her
lowest score ever.

She didn't realize how worried she must
have looked until Mr. Garcia took her paper
and asked, "Are you feeling all right, Señorita
Stewart?"

"I—uh, sure, I'm fine," she stammered.
Then, remembering he liked them to answer
his questions in Spanish, she translated,
"Estoy bien, gracias, Señor Garcia."

She liked her Spanish teacher. He was a plump man with a shiny bald spot and a bushy, black mustache that always smelled of his pipe tobacco, but he was really very nice and always took extra time to go over things.

She stared at his pipe lying on his desk, thinking how strange it was that a day that had started out so wonderfully could end up so lousy. Actually, she *was* a little queasy—like after a ride on a roller coaster.

"Tomorrow I want you to turn in your translations for chapter five of *Gaucho Smith*," he was telling the class. "That is, if you can keep your minds off genies long enough to concentrate on gauchos."

He was staring directly at Kerrie again, a broad smile lifting the ends of his mustache. "I hear you created quite a commotion in school this morning with your genie, Señorita Stewart. When a sensible girl like you gets carried away like that, I know things have really gotten out of hand."

A sensible girl like me . . .

Kerrie felt anything but sensible. In fact, her feelings were so twisted, she didn't see how she would ever untangle them. Mike *did* seem to like her, in spite of the abrupt way he'd deserted her at lunch. But did he like her in the same way she liked him? Maybe not now—but could he if she gave him the chance? Was it worth risking her grades to find out? For if things continued to go the way they were, she'd be lucky if she could concentrate long enough to add two and two.

When the bell rang, she wasn't any closer to the answer, and the thought of facing Mike again sent her stomach somersaulting.

Chapter Six

Allison and Jill had taken off early in Allison's Datsun, so Kerrie was waiting in front of school for the bus when a battered VW bug swerved to a stop at the curb. A familiar curly head poked out the window on the driver's side.

"Need a ride, Kerrie?" Mike called. "There's not much room, but I'm sure we can find a spare lap for you to sit on."

The backseat of the tiny car was jammed, and Marcy sat in front, enthroned like a haughty queen in the bucket seat next to Mike. Kerrie hesitated. After the scene in the cafeteria, she had no desire to be around Marcy—and Marcy's expression told her the feeling was more than mutual.

"Come on," Mike urged. "We're going to the

Stagestop first. It'll be fun—we'd like it if you came along."

She noticed how he used the word "we" in front of Marcy, but his smile was so warm and persuasive, she couldn't refuse him. "OK, why not?"

Marcy didn't budge, so Mike got out to let her in on his side. He pushed the seat forward while she squeezed in between two pairs of lanky legs, one in gym shorts, the other in Levi's with holes in the knees.

"Kerrie, you know Jim and Eric and Laura, don't you?" Mike introduced breezily.

She nodded. She recognized Jim Schumaker from art class. He was tall like Mike, but stockier, and had short black hair. A pair of dark-lashed, gray eyes met hers as she settled in beside him as well as she could. It was an embarrassingly tight fit; she could feel the ribs of his corded Levis pressing into her leg on one side, and Eric grunted loudly as he tried to give her room on the other side and hit his back on the window crank.

Kerrie had never met Eric Berger before, but everyone knew he was on the basketball team and that he was Laura Patterson's steady. Laura sat on his lap, one arm twined around his neck. She greeted Kerrie with an icy hello.

"Hi, everybody," Kerrie mumbled, wishing now she hadn't agreed to come. She didn't fit in with any of these people—in more ways than one.

"Kerrie's the one who got me thinking I might sign up for summer school," Mike said, dropping into a lower gear to help the chattering engine out through the parking-lot gates. "My job at the print shop's only going to be afternoons, so I figure it won't hurt to go to school in the morning. Maybe I won't get to college, but at least I'll know I didn't go down without a fight."

"Look who's getting serious all of a sudden!" Eric exclaimed, hooting. "I thought all you were interested in was playing it for laughs."

"Can't be a genie all my life, can I?" Mike asked. "Last time I checked the want ads, there wasn't a big demand for them."

"Summer school's a drag, Mike," Marcy interjected. "Besides, I was hoping you could get away for a week to spend some time with us up at Clear Lake. Mom and Dad will be disappointed if you can't come. You know how crazy Mom is about you; in fact, if she were any younger, I think I'd be jealous!"

So, thought Kerrie, she had Marcy's parents to contend with as well! She had a feeling the remark was made especially for her benefit. It was getting more complicated by the minute.

"Gee, I don't know, Marcy. I'll have to see . . ."

Laura changed the subject. "What did you think of Skeeter Hollis today? Didn't he crack you up?"

Skeeter had shown up at school wearing a moth-eaten 1940s evening gown his master had picked out for him at a thrift shop. On his skinny, six-foot-four frame, with size fourteen sneakers completing the ensemble, he'd managed to steal the show from most of the other genies.

Jim moaned. "All I can say is, I'm glad it was him and not me."

"Come on, Schumaker, I'll bet you'd look sensational in that outfit," Eric teased. "Remember the time at Ben's party when . . ."

Suddenly he was launching into a story that included everyone—except Kerrie. She felt silly, cramped in next to these kids. Whether they meant to or not, they had succeeded in excluding her from their tight-knit group. It hadn't been that way at lunch with Mike and *her* friends. But was that only because he made more of an effort to join in? she asked herself. Whatever the reason, she breathed a sigh of relief when the Stagestop came into sight.

One by one, they all climbed out, made their way inside, and headed for an empty booth. Marcy slid in quickly next to Mike, as Jim smiled and made room for Kerrie. He even asked her a few questions about school—which he did only out of politeness, she was sure. They gave their food orders, but Kerrie ordered just a Pepsi, since her stomach still felt upset.

When the food was served, Marcy looked at Kerrie's Pepsi and inquired sweetly, "You're on a diet, too?"

"You women and your diets!" Mike interjected. "Kerrie doesn't need to diet—she looks just fine to me."

From Marcy's look, Kerrie could see that she had scored a point without even trying. *Serves her right for being so catty!* she thought. Not to be outdone, however, Marcy pushed her hamburger aside after one bite, declaring that she was full.

"I hear the dance committee is getting that new western group, Hay Fever, for Saturday night," Laura mentioned.

"Somehow I wonder how a group of cowboys is going to sound in a gym decorated as the Den of the Forty Thieves!" Eric said laughing.

"Who cares as long as they're good?" Mike asked. He picked up a straw and blew the wrapper across the table, where it landed in the middle of Jim's french-fried onion rings.

Conversation continued about the dance for the next few minutes, while Kerrie silently sipped her drink. Who was wearing what, who was going with whom, who *wasn't* going with whom. . . .

"I wonder if Bob's taking Skeeter as his date?" Jim asked, causing everyone to collapse in laughter.

Unexpectedly, Laura turned to Kerrie and asked, "Who are you going with?"

Kerrie could feel the heat climbing up into her cheeks. She should have known something like this was going to happen!

"I"—she searched wildly for an answer— "don't think you'd know him. He—he goes to Atherton High," she finished lamely.

"Oh?" Marcy showed interest in her for the first time. "What's his name? I have a cousin who goes to Atherton, maybe she knows him."

"Actually, I don't remember his name," Kerrie said, quickly inventing. "He's a friend of Allison's brother, and I've never met him."

"How cute—a blind date!" Laura exclaimed.

"I've never had one myself, but I'll bet it'd be fun. Kind of like Christmas, you don't know what you're getting until you open the package."

For some reason, Laura seemed to find her remark terribly funny and went into a fit of hysterical giggling. To Kerrie, it seemed obvious they were laughing at her. She was positive they knew she'd made the whole thing up.

Luckily, Mike sensed her discomfort and announced that they'd better take off since he had to pick his brother up from soccer practice.

A few minutes later, they were all sardined back into the bug, heading down Glenwood Road to drop Laura and Eric off at Eric's house. Jim lived only a few blocks away, and soon there were only Mike, Marcy, and Kerrie left. Kerrie thought of the old saying: "Two's company, three's a crowd." If anyone could make her feel like a crowd, it would be Marcy.

Kerrie told Mike where she lived. "Hey, that's not far from my house," Mike said. "In fact, it's on the way, so it won't be any trouble to drop you off. We have to take a detour first, though, because Marcy really lives out in the boondocks."

"Why don't I just come over to your house?" Marcy suggested in a silky voice, trailing her fingertips along the back of Mike's neck. "I'm sure Kerrie wants to get home, and I can always get a ride home later."

"Gee, Marcy, I'd like that—except, you see, I sort of promised Kurt I'd take him to an early movie after dinner."

"No problem, I'll just go with you. It'll be fun."

"*Attack of the Space Spiders* fun? You've got to be kidding! I wouldn't put anyone else through that kind of torture, believe me."

Marcy pouted, but at least she knew when to shut up. When Mike pulled into her driveway, she kissed him on the cheek before getting out. "I guess I *could* use the time to work on my dress," she admitted. "Just wait until you see it! I can tell you right now, it'll knock you off your feet."

"In that case, does it come with an insurance policy?" Mike asked jokingly.

I'll have to remember that one to tell to my dad, Kerrie thought, smiling to herself. She climbed into the seat Marcy had vacated and noticed that Marcy was frowning as she turned away.

On impulse, Kerrie called out cheerily, "See you, Marcy!"

Startled, Marcy looked back over her shoulder. "Oh, right, see ya, Kerrie," she tossed back with obvious reluctance.

Score two, Kerrie told herself; coming out of her shell was turning out to be more fun than she had imagined. Mike pulled away, and it was finally just the two of them.

Chapter Seven

"Old Johannsen really got a kick out of our stunt this morning," Mike commented as they started up the winding mountain road that would eventually take them to Kerrie's house. "First time I've ever seen her smile. Too bad she wasn't around for our big encore in art— she probably would have fainted!"

"Oh, she's not so bad once you get to know her," Kerrie said.

"Maybe she's nice to you—and I can see why. Unfortunately I came within a hair of flunking history last semester. I'm not on her list of favorite students."

"I wouldn't feel bad. From what I hear you're not the only one."

"Well, I can't really blame her. It's my own fault. Every time I even look at a history book,

I end up falling asleep. Somehow, I just can't get too excited over what year they signed the Magna Carta."

Kerrie laughed. "I know what you mean. Some of it *is* pretty boring."

"I'll bet you got an A anyway," he said.

"A-minus," she corrected, realizing as she said it how silly the difference would sound to someone like Mike. "I don't think she was too crazy about the term paper I wrote on why George Washington never smiled."

"Why didn't he?"

"Well, for one thing, he had this terrible case of carbuncles on his rear end, so you can imagine what he was feeling like every time he sat down for someone to paint his portrait."

Mike threw his head back and roared with laughter. "You're really funny, you know that, Kerrie—in a nice sort of way."

His compliment made her feel warm all over. "Speaking of history, have you ever been inside the Glenwood Museum?"

"That's off the road just up ahead, isn't it?" Mike asked. "The old-time general store? I think we went there once on a field trip when I was in grammar school. Funny how you can live right near something and drive past it every day, but you forget it's there after a while."

"I thought if you weren't in too much of a

hurry, maybe you'd like to stop in and take a quick look around. It's really interesting. Maybe you'd change your mind about history being so dull after you've seen it."

"Sure, why not? Kurt's soccer practice doesn't let out for another half hour. I guess it won't hurt to give history another shot." He gave her a playful wink. "As long as I've got you for a guide instead of old Johannsen."

A few minutes later they were pulling into the graveled parking lot next to a hitching post and moss-covered wooden horse trough. Even though it was getting late, the sun was pleasantly warm as it filtered through the lacy canopy of oak trees overhead.

Inside the museum, it was darker and quite a bit cooler. "Hi, Mrs. Winthrop," Kerrie greeted the elderly caretaker, who lived in a tiny modern house behind the original nineteenth-century building.

"Nice to see you again, Kerrie!" she said, smiling. "It's been a while. And I see you've brought your young man along. My, it certainly *has* been a while."

Kerrie blushed, realizing that Mrs. Winthrop thought Mike was her boyfriend. Kerrie made the introductions, and then proceeded to show Mike around the tiny store, preserved as it would have been a century before.

"Hey, this stuff is really interesting!" he exclaimed, stopping to examine a cluster of plows and other antique farm equipment.

They looked at an early model, hand-powered washing machine with a wringer, an iron that had to be heated on a stove before clothes could be pressed, pretty porcelain chamber pots, even an old tin shower stall over which buckets of water were poured. Kerrie could hardly tear Mike away from a dusty, dilapidated printing press.

"Mom ought to see this," he said. "She thinks *her* equipment is outdated."

"Mrs. Winthrop calls this a slice of living history," she remarked. "When I was little I didn't understand what she meant by slice, and I used to wander around trying to find where the cake was hidden."

Mike chuckled softly. "What an imagination! But that doesn't surprise me after the way you came through today. In case I forgot to mention it, that was really a super stunt you thought up. I'm lucky to have such a clever master."

Kerrie steered him to a roped-off section with a counter and pigeonhole cabinet marked "Glenwood General Delivery." A mannequin, outfitted in an authentic bustled dress with a beaded handbag dangling from her wrist, completed the setting.

"In the old days the store had to double as a post office, too," she explained.

Mike gave a low whistle of appreciation. "Do you know, my family has lived in Glenwood since my grandmother was a little girl? I'll bet she even used to shop here. I guess I just never thought much about it until now. Wow! Did I say history was dull?"

Kerrie stopped to admire a lovely brass kerosene lamp. "Do you think if I rubbed it a genie might pop out and grant me three wishes?" she asked mischievously.

"Trying to put me out of a job, huh? That's gratitude for you!"

"It's pretty, though, don't you think? If I had one like it, I know just where I'd put it." She was thinking of the marble-topped oak washstand she and her mother had bought at an auction last summer. They had stripped and refinished it to go in Kerrie's bedroom.

"Don't I get a say in this? After all, I mean if I'm going to be living inside it . . ."

"Forget it, Mike, you wouldn't fit."

"You've got a point there."

"Look over here," she said. "I've saved the best for last." She guided him to a glass case that had once served as a candy counter. There was one jar still sitting on top.

"What are those things inside?" he wanted to know.

"You'll never guess!"

"They look like marbles, except they're all lopsided."

"They're hundred-year-old jelly beans!"

Mike peered closely in amazement. "No kidding? I wonder what they taste like now."

Kerrie giggled. "Why don't you try one and see?"

He gave her a look that sent them both into fits of hysterical giggling. Mrs. Winthrop glanced up from the magazine she was reading to give them a wistful smile. She shook her head, murmuring, "You young people . . ."

They had what Kerrie's mother called the "sillies." Whenever they managed to stop laughing, one of them would start and get the other one going again. Mike and Kerrie were doubled over all the way to the car; they kept giving in to spurts of laughter on the way home.

"What a pair we make!" Mike said in a sputter. "Between the two of us, we should be able to dream up a few more stunts like today's." He paused. "Hey, I know! Maybe I could carry Mrs. Johannsen through the halls on my shoulders. That would sure get everyone's attention!"

The idea sent them into fresh gales of laughter. Before they knew it, Mike was pulling up in front of her house, a redwood-paneled ranch at the bottom of a circular drive, artistically framed by ground ivy, creeping up over boulders, and splaying ferns and trees.

"Would you like to come in for a minute?" she asked. "I could probably find a glass of juice or something."

"Sounds tempting, but I really better get going, or I'll be late. You never know what Kurt's going to do—take off for the moon, maybe. Some other time, huh?"

"Sure . . . thanks for the ride, Mike."

She was opening the car door when she felt a firm hand on her shoulder. She turned to see Mike smiling at her, not a joking smile, but a real honest-to-goodness one. His eyes seemed full of sparkling green and gold lights, making her feel as if she were floating under water. She felt a little lightheaded, and her stomach was doing somersaults again.

"I had a good time, Kerrie," he said softly. "I mean it. You're really fun to be with, you know."

"Me, too," she answered, averting her face, so he wouldn't see how much his words meant to her. She was holding her breath, wondering if the magic would hold out long enough for him to ask her out.

It doesn't have to be the dance, Mike . . . a movie will do just fine. I'll even sit through Attack of the Space Spiders *if you want me to.*

He didn't ask her, but she wasn't too disappointed, since she hadn't really expected him to. One step at a time, she cautioned herself. It *was* a special day. He couldn't go on thinking of her as dull and serious now.

"See you tomorrow," she sang out on her way up the front path of sunken redwood rounds. "And be prepared—I may have another trick or two up my sleeve."

"I wouldn't be surprised," he tossed back, grinning as he drove off with a roar and clunking of gears.

Neither would I, thought Kerrie, giving a little skip as she ran into the house.

Chapter Eight

"So, tell us poor peasants what it feels like to have your very own genie," Kerrie's father teased as they sat around the big oak table at dinner.

"Better than I expected," Kerrie said, helping herself to a second ear of corn and smearing it with butter. She was suddenly ravenous. "It's kind of nice, actually."

"Just so long as it doesn't spoil you," her mother said smiling. "Unless Mike wants to come over and do the dishes, looks like you're stuck with them tonight."

Leslie eyed the corn longingly. She couldn't eat it because it got stuck in her braces, so she scooped up a spoonful of mashed potatoes instead.

"I saw him eating lunch with you today,"

she mentioned to her sister. "He's really cute. Has he asked you out yet?"

Trust Les to get right to the heart of the matter! "We're just friends," she answered carefully, wiping melted butter from her chin.

"Some friend! I saw the way he was looking at you." She sighed. "Isn't it romantic? *My* sister and the Robert Redford of Glenwood High—"

Kerrie squirmed as she felt her parents' eyes on her.

"Cut it out, Les. I'm surprised you can see past the end of your nose, the way you've been daydreaming over Robbie."

"I have not!" she protested, but the pink in her cheeks was a dead giveaway. Abruptly she changed the subject. "What time is it, Dad?"

Mr. Stewart gave a knowing smile as he glanced at his wristwatch. He was a husky man with thinning blond hair and blue eyes like Kerrie's.

"Don't worry," he said. "The countdown hasn't begun yet. It's a whole hour more before the inquisition begins, so you might as well relax and finish your dinner."

Leslie groaned. "Please, Dad, you're not going to ask Robbie a whole bunch of embarrassing questions, are you? I'll just die!"

Kerrie smiled at her sister's dramatics—no wonder she fit in so well with the kids in the Players' Guild!

"If you die, Les, who's Robbie going to take to the dance?" she wanted to know.

In answer, Leslie stuck out her tongue.

"Have some more salad, dear," Mrs. Stewart put in mildly. She was used to their antics.

"Uh, Mom—" Kerrie thought she might as well come right out with it. "Would you mind if I invited someone over for dinner Friday night?"

Mrs. Stewart looked up in surprise. "Friday's your birthday! This 'someone' wouldn't perhaps be a boy?"

Kerrie flushed. "I was thinking of asking Mike."

"Does he know it's your birthday?"

"I won't tell him *that*. I just thought it might be a good night to have him over, since you're cooking a special dinner and all."

This year she particularly didn't want to make a big deal about her birthday. According to some people, sixteen was supposed to be a kind of magical number when all sorts of wonderful things started to happen. And Kerrie still wasn't sure if she believed in magic or not. With Mike, it was too soon to tell. She especially didn't want him to know it was her birthday, or he might feel obligated to get her a present.

Friday night was perfect, though, as far as dinner was concerned. At least they wouldn't have warmed-over squash casserole—in spite of what Mike said about health food, she didn't think he was quite ready for that! Her mother had promised to make her favorite meal— lasagne with spinach noodles, parsley pota- toes, and a banana cake for dessert.

"It's all right with me, Kerrie," she said, "if that's what you want."

"Two in one week!" Dad complained. "I'm not sure I'm ready for this. Next thing you know they'll be putting me out to pasture."

Mrs. Stewart gave him a sharp glance. "In that case, you can plan on grazing alone. I'm going to lead a very active old age!"

Paying no attention to her parents' banter- ing, Leslie said to Kerrie, "Robbie told me that Russ Monteith had to go to the faculty lounge at lunch and shine everyone's shoes, but I heard that you and Mike were the big attraction. Robbie saw you out in the quad in those costumes and could hardly believe it. I didn't believe it myself." Her blue eyes twinkled. "I told him it must have been some- one who looked like my sister."

"Thanks a heap," Kerrie shot back good-naturedly, nibbling the last few kernels from her cob. "Seriously, I'm going to have to come up with something else soon, now that my fans are expecting it. Ah, the demands of stardom!"

"Aargh!" Leslie choked, recovering a moment later to suggest, "Why not make him do something romantic? You know, you could have him pick you a bunch of flowers or something."

Kerrie moaned loudly. "That's the worst idea I've ever heard! You sound just like Jill."

"You know," Dad began thoughtfully, "when I was going through my fraternity initiation, they had us go around campus on a scavenger hunt. It was really something, though— we had to collect things like a hair from Dean Thornton's toupee and a nylon stocking from the sorority next door—"

"Ted!" Mrs. Stewart broke in. "You never told me."

He smiled mysteriously. "A man's entitled to *some* secrets."

Meanwhile, something clicked in Kerrie's head. A scavenger hunt! It was so ordinary, and yet . . . if she could make it *un*ordinary, the way her dad had described it, it could be sensational. She decided it would give Mike and a few other people a chance to see what she could do besides making A's.

"Dad, you're brilliant." She pushed her chair back, ignoring his confused look, then dashed for her room.

Kerrie pulled the phone in and shut the door. She dialed Jill's number, knowing Allison was out with Kevin on a study date at the library. Besides, with her exaggerated imagination, Jill was just the one to help her out.

Jill answered on the second ring.

"Hi, Jill. Kerrie. Can you come over now? It's important."

Jill sighed noisily. "It better be. I'm just getting to the good part in *Blazing Bold Passion*—where he beats up the guy who kidnapped her, and now he's untying her—"

"Sounds thrilling. But this is even better. I've got an idea for a genie stunt, and I need your help."

"I'll be right over!"

Jill arrived fifteen minutes later. Kerrie poured a couple glasses of milk and grabbed a handful of cookies to take into her room.

"A scavenger hunt?" Jill nodded thoughtfully after Kerrie had told her the idea. "I like it! Simple but clever. We can't make it too easy, though."

"That's why I called you. So far I've only thought up one item."

Kerrie rummaged in her desk drawer for a note pad and pencil. She wrote down:

1) One perfect blond hair from Jaynie Cox's head.

Jill giggled. "Serve her right for always being so perfect. Perfection makes me nauseous." She gulped her milk and bit into a cookie.

"Got any other ideas?" Kerrie asked hopefully.

"Hmmm." Jill munched her cookie thoughtfully. "How about one of Skeeter Hollis's sneakers? We could always use it as a rubber life raft if we ever go boating."

Kerrie wrote it down and added underneath:

3) A pair of gym shorts from the girls' locker room.

4) A pinch of tobacco from Mr. Garcia's pipe.

Jill peered over her shoulder. "Hey, those are good. I wish I could be there to see Mike's face when you show him."

"Come on, let's think of some more. I want to make this really hard for him."

An hour later, they had a list of twenty items, including a plastic geranium from the vase on Mrs. Feltham's desk—she taught world geography—an aspirin from the nurse's office, a football decal from Pete Scanlon's locker door, and a whisker off Wilbur the Wildcat, Glenwood's mascot.

"Kerrie, I've got to hand it to you—this is a fantastic idea. Mike's going to love it after he gets through hating it. And Marcy will be positively *green*."

"The way she looked at me when Mike and I left her off this afternoon, I'll be surprised if I don't get a knife in my back tomorrow."

"Well, you know what they say about jealousy."

"What?"

"It's a good sign you're getting somewhere if someone is jealous of you. Marcy wouldn't be so catty if she didn't consider you competition."

Kerry fell back on the bed, hugging a pillow to her chest. "You're forgetting one minor detail, aren't you? Mike's taking Marcy to the dance, not me."

"That doesn't prove anything. He asked her before he got to know you."

"I just remembered something." Kerrie made a strangling sound as she rolled over. "I told them I had a date for the dance. I was so desperate, I never thought. . . . They'll know I was lying when I don't show up!"

Jill frowned as she scoured the last crumbs from the plate. "I guess you can just tell them you were sick or something," she said lamely.

"How did I ever get into this mess?" Kerrie asked.

"You had a little help from your friends, remember?"

"How could I forget?"

Jill's merry expression grew sober. "Just do me one favor, Ker. Don't let Marcy or that dumb Laura Patterson get you down, OK?"

Kerrie sighed. "I'll try not to. I just wish—I wish I could be more sure of how Mike feels about me. I mean, he hasn't said anything, really. Except he told me I was fun to be with."

"That's a good start. Give him a chance, will you? It's only been a couple of days. Even in books you've got to give the guy until chapter fifteen or so."

"You're sooo reassuring, Jill." Kerrie leaped

up from the bed, still hugging her pillow, and started waltzing around the room. "Here, I'd like you to meet my fabulous date for the dance. His name is—Freddie Fiberfill."

Jill snorted in disgust. "Thanks, but we've already met. In fact, we're old friends."

The two collapsed back on the bed in giggles.

Robbie arrived as Jill was leaving. He looked so nervous that Kerrie wondered if his glasses were going to start fogging up. He was short, only a couple of inches taller than Leslie, with dark brown hair that curled around his ears, and an infectious grin.

Leslie nervously made the introductions, but when she got to Kerrie, Robbie said, "Hi, Kerrie. Heard about you and Mike today in history."

Kerrie grinned. "Wait until you find out what I've cooked up for Mike next."

Her parents exchanged looks that seemed to say, *Is this our Kerrie?*

Mr. Stewart extended Robbie his hand. "Leslie tells me you're on the soccer team," he said, guiding him into the living room. "I used to play a bit of soccer myself in college. . . ."

Robbie's nervousness had vanished, and he was talking about school sports when

Kerrie left them. Leslie couldn't have looked more delighted if Superman had swooped down out of the sky to save the day. Kerrie wasn't the least bit envious of her sister's happiness. She had too much on her mind for that.

Chapter Nine

On Wednesday, Kerrie didn't catch up with Mike until art. She tracked him down behind a stack of poster boards, where he was busy cutting up pieces of colored tissue paper for a collage, and showed him the scavenger list.

Mike grimaced in mock horror when he finished reading it. "Wow, Kerrie, you must think I have real magical powers or something. I'm going to have to find a way to walk through walls to get some of this stuff!"

"If anyone can, you'll find a way," she told him. Two days ago, she wouldn't have had the nerve to insist.

He grinned at her. "You really have an evil mind, you know that?"

"How sweet of you to notice, Mike."

"Seriously, Kerrie, I'll bet no one's ever thought of anything like this before."

"You really think it's good?"

"I know it is." He began laying some of the tissue paper on the board so that the pieces overlapped. Then he brushed them with a gluelike varnish. "What are we going to do with all that stuff when I find it, though? We have to have some way of showing it off at the parade."

Watching him work on the collage gave her an idea.

"I've got it," she said. "We'll make a display— on a big piece of poster board like that one. Most of the things can be glued or pinned on. We can write a bunch of captions to go with them."

Mike stared at her so long she felt embarrassed. "You're a genius, Kerrie. A real genius."

It wasn't exactly the kind of compliment she would have preferred, but it would have to do until something better came along. Actually, if someone had told her a week ago that she'd be huddled in a corner sharing secrets with Mike Price, she'd have thought that person was crazy. Now it seemed perfectly normal for her to be talking to him, even joking with him.

"If you hear any bloodcurdling screams

today," he went on, "you'll know it's just me going about my business. I have a feeling I'll be making more than a few enemies this week."

"Let's not tell anyone what you're doing until the parade, OK?" she said. "Let's make it a surprise."

"A kind of Glenwood Hall of Fame? Sure, that sounds great. You can count on me."

"You know, Mike"—she stared down at the floor, gathering her courage—"I didn't know how this was going to work out when we first started, but I want you to know—"

"That we make a good team?" he supplied. "Sure! Kind of like Laurel and Hardy."

She laughed. "More like the two stooges."

It wasn't exactly what she'd meant to say— what she wanted to tell him, but couldn't get herself to say, was how much she liked being with him, all genie business aside. More and more she was discovering that, beneath the surface, they really did have things in common. Mike was a warm, caring person—and intelligent, in spite of the way he was always putting himself down about his grades.

"What are you making the collage for?" she asked with sudden interest. She knew it wasn't one of their class assignments.

For the first time, Mike appeared unsure of

himself. "You'll never believe this, but it's for one of my mom's customers. He's got this sport shop downtown, and he needs some posters to advertise this big sale he's going to have."

"That's wonderful, Mike!" Kerrie was sincerely enthused. "I didn't know you were interested in advertising."

She noticed the tips of his ears were turning a bright shade of pink. "Yeah, well . . . I sort of got into it after my mother bought the shop. I'm not sure if I'm any good at it yet, but I like to fool around with it."

"I'll bet you *are* good at it. Is that why you want to go to summer school?"

"I hear some of the state colleges have some pretty good courses in journalism and advertising. I'd sure like to give it a try." His expression was shy. "You don't think it's crazy, do you?"

"Of course I don't! How can you know what you want to do, or if you're good at something, until you've tried it?"

She remembered her mother's advice about the importance of a good education and was momentarily chagrined that she'd argued with her about it.

He smiled sheepishly. "Somehow I figured you'd understand, Kerrie. When I told Marcy, she—" he broke off with a shrug and was suddenly his old bantering self again. "Oh, well, not everyone recognizes raw talent when they see it."

He pasted two triangular pieces, one on top of the other, to create a pinkish shade of orange, then stood back. "Now that's what I call a masterpiece. Look out, Michelangelo, here I come!"

Before the bell rang, Mr. Mueller called for everyone to start cleaning up. Kerrie put away the ink sketch she'd been working on and helped Mike pick up the scraps of tissue paper that littered the floor like confetti. Jim Schumaker passed by on his way to the sink with some purple-coated paint brushes and stopped to greet them.

"You gonna be at the Stagestop after school, Kerrie?" he inquired casually.

"I can't go," she said. She started to add that she was behind on some of her homework and had to get home early so she could study, but something stopped her. Somehow, she didn't think it was the sort of excuse either of the boys was used to hearing. "I—I promised my mother I'd help her with some things around the house."

"Oh, well, I was just wondering." Jim's ears were red as he sauntered off.

"I think you've made a conquest," Mike whispered to her, his eyes sparkling. "Jim told me this morning that it was too bad you already had a date for the dance, or he would have asked you to go with him."

"Me?" she asked with a gasp, then immediately afterward could have kicked herself for acting so surprised.

"What's so strange about that? I'll bet you have guys beating down your door all the time."

"Oh, yeah." She managed a shaky laugh, "Hundreds of them."

But all I want is one. She couldn't help being disappointed that Mike hadn't seemed even a little bit jealous. And how did she feel about Jim wanting to ask her to the dance? She was certainly stunned—and, she thought, if she were to be honest with herself, she was also flattered.

It was nice to discover that guys noticed her, thought Kerrie. Maybe all it took was a little self-confidence and a smile. And a chance to show someone what she was really like. She had learned to let down some of her barriers lately, and it seemed to be paying off.

She wondered what she would say if Jim asked her out. Should she go? She didn't know him very well, but he seemed nice. Last year, she recalled, he'd dated Cathy Hobbs, one of the most popular girls in their class.

She knew what Allison would say: "A bird in the hand is worth two in the bush." How long should she wait for Mike to make the first move? Would he ever ask her out, or did he just want to be friends? She wondered if this was the right time to bring up the subject of dinner at her house. Well, she decided, no other time was going to be any better.

"I asked my mom about dinner," she began, as the bell rang, and they were pushed out into the corridor. "Does Friday night sound OK?"

She held her breath until she heard him say, "Sure, sounds great. What time?"

"We usually eat around six-thirty."

"Good. That'll give me time to warm up a pizza for Kurt. I can drop him off at his friend David's house on the way over. David's as weird as he is, so he's always happy when I leave him there."

Kerrie's mind was already soaring ahead to Friday night, so she didn't see the stack of lumber for the new bleachers they were building in the gym. She would have tripped if Mike hadn't grabbed her hand to steer her out of the way.

"Looks like you need a genie just to watch out for you," he teased, not letting go of her hand.

Kerrie was thrilled by the warmth of his firm grip. She could feel her arm tingling all the way up to her elbow and her face was heating up dangerously.

Hand in hand, they walked past the swimming pool, which was wedged between the girls' and the boys' locker rooms. A small crowd was gathered outside the fence, and everyone seemed to be laughing.

"What's going on over there?" wondered Kerrie.

They went over to have a look and saw Randy Cooke bobbing around the pool in a giant inner tube clutching a fishing pole. Everyone cheered encouragingly as he began furiously cranking the reel, pretending to fight the line, before finally hauling in his prize—a rubber swim fin—which he added to the growing pile of bathing caps, snorkels, and face masks by the side of the pool.

"Whoever masterminded that one deserves credit," Kerrie remarked. "I can see we've got some pretty stiff competition."

Mike squeezed her hand, giving her a look that made her feel all warm and wobbly. "I have a feeling you and I will do all right."

Allison accosted Kerrie on her way to lunch.

"Jill told me about the scavenger hunt," she said, "I think it's a fantastic idea. I saw Mike sneaking up on Jaynie Cox a few minutes ago, and it's a good thing I knew what was going on, or I would have believed what everyone says about him being such an awful flirt."

Kerrie stopped and looked at her friend. "I never heard anyone say that about Mike."

Allison turned red. "Oh, Kerrie, me and my big mouth! It's just a stupid rumor I heard, and I had to go and repeat it. Anyway, I'm sure it's not true."

"He's just friendlier than most people, so I guess I can see how someone would think that." She wasn't going to let anything get in the way of her wonderful mood. Not even Marcy could do that at the moment.

Allison prattled on about Kevin, their date the night before, his basketball practice this afternoon. "Are you going to the game tomorrow night?" she asked. "Mike's playing."

"Oh, I don't know." Kerrie had never had much of an interest in sports, and after asking Mike over for dinner, she didn't want to give him the idea she was chasing him by showing up wherever he went. "I'll think about it, Al."

"You should take more of an interest in the things Mike likes," she chided. "How long do you think Kevin would hang around if I yawned every time he talked about basketball?"

Kerrie shook her head and laughed. "Mike and I haven't gotten to that point yet."

"I'm glad to see you finally admit you *are* going somewhere with him."

"Maybe—I'm not sure yet."

"For heaven's sake, Kerrie! Do you have to be hit over the head with a baseball bat?"

"It really is too soon to tell," Kerrie insisted. "This week he's my genie—I know he likes me, but . . ."

After Genie Week, when he was free to choose, what would she be to him?

"It's only Wednesday," Allison reminded her. "A lot could happen between now and Friday."

And not all of it good. Kerrie couldn't stop the uneasy thought from creeping in.

Chapter Ten

"Hold still," Kerrie commanded. "If you keep wiggling, I'll end up sticking you with this pin."

She was beginning to wish now she'd never agreed to help Leslie hem her formal. Their mother had volunteered to do it, but Kerrie insisted on helping. The sky-blue color exactly matched Leslie's eyes, and Kerrie had to admit she looked gorgeous in it.

"I'm trying," Leslie insisted. "But every time I think about Robbie putting his arms around me and sweeping me onto the dance floor, I get all jumpy."

"Nerves," Kerrie stated with the assurance of an expert. It was exactly the same feeling she had whenever she thought about Mike.

Leslie launched into theatrics once more.

"Well, what if I faint or something? They'll have to carry me out on a stretcher, and Robbie will be so embarrassed he'll never speak to me again!"

"I can see the headlines in Sunday's paper already," Kerrie said, playing along: " 'Tragedy Mars Teen Prom.' " She slid a pin through the silky fabric, accidentally sticking her finger. "Ouch! Now look what you made me do."

Leslie managed to look sorry. "OK, OK, I guess I do get a little carried away sometimes."

"That's the understatement of the year!"

Kerrie finished pinning the hem, then stood back while Leslie twirled about in front of the full-length mirror on her bedroom door. Her eyes sparkled, and her cheeks were flushed.

"Do you think Robbie will like it?" she asked breathlessly.

"I think they'll have to carry *him* out on a stretcher."

Impulsively, Leslie hugged her. "Oh, Kerrie, I wish you were going, too!"

"So do I," Kerrie admitted out loud for the first time.

Somehow she didn't feel quite so bad about it knowing that she might have at least gone with Jim, if she hadn't made up that stupid story at the Stagestop.

"I'll survive," she added firmly. "Your older sister isn't entirely hopeless, you know."

"Of course not, I never thought you were! You're so pretty and smart and everything. Sometimes I get so jealous, I—"

"Wait a minute," Kerrie broke in. "*You* get jealous of *me*?"

Leslie stared at herself in the mirror with disgust. "Uh-oh, now I've done it. You'll never let me forget I said that."

"I promise I'll never mention it again, scouts' honor."

She eyed Kerrie suspiciously. "You were never a Girl Scout."

"Oh, for heaven's sake—!"

"All right, I meant it. You *are* pretty, Kerrie, even if you don't always know it. And I don't have to tell you how smart you are—everybody knows that."

"You really think I'm pretty?" Kerrie unzipped the dress and helped her sister wriggle out of it. When her head finally emerged from all the yards of ruffled blue fabric, Leslie eyed her thoughtfully.

"Yes, I do. But if I say something, you promise not to get mad?"

"How can I promise that until I know what it is?"

"Well . . . I think you'd be a lot prettier if you wore your hair differently."

"What's wrong with it?" Kerrie peered closely in the mirror, examining her brown hair, which was parted in the middle and hung straight down to her shoulders. A tiny frown formed between her blue eyes. "I've always worn it this way."

"That's just what I mean. You've worn it the same old way since you were in the fourth grade. Don't you want to try something a little more grown-up now that you're turning sixteen?"

"Why do I get this sudden image from *Bride of Frankenstein*?" Kerrie quipped.

Leslie shrugged and sat down at the dressing table, making an elaborate show of filing her nails. "Well, if you don't *want* to look your best for Mike, it's all right with me!"

Kerrie threw up her hands in surrender. Maybe Leslie was right. Maybe it was time for a change. "All right, what do you suggest, Herr Doctor?"

Three hours later, after a trip to Rexall's for a home-perm kit, Kerrie sat nervously before her dressing-table mirror while Leslie uncoiled the last sponge roller from her hair, which had been trimmed by several inches. She never would have submitted to this whole thing if she hadn't trusted Leslie's instincts when it came to hairstyling. Her younger sister had been experimenting with hair ever since she had gotten her first doll and had done a creditable job on several of her friends so far. No wonder she wanted to go to a beauty school after she graduated from high school.

Leslie brushed Kerrie's hair into smooth, shiny waves that curled about her face, giving her a soft, delicate look.

"Ta-*dah*!" She took a step backward to admire her handiwork. "Now what do you say?"

Kerrie didn't know what to say. It was . . . perfect. She turned her head to one side, admiring the way the silky curls fell about her neck without looking stiff or unnatural. She grinned at her reflection in the mirror. In more ways than one, she felt like a butterfly that had finally crawled out of its cocoon.

"You were right, Les," she confessed. "It's beautiful."

"I'll bet Mike thinks so, too," Leslie shot back. "He's coming over on Friday, isn't he?"

"The last I heard."

"I'll bet when he finds out it's your birthday, he'll want to take you somewhere really special after dinner."

"You think so?" She hadn't thought of it before, but before she knew it, her imagination was off and running. Why not? It didn't even have to be someplace special. He could take her to a movie, maybe just for a drive. She laughed at herself. "I don't know what you did to me, Les, but I'm even beginning to think like you."

Leslie grinned. "I'm glad to see *some* good came of it."

Kerrie picked up one of the foam curlers and tossed it at her. By the time Mrs. Stewart poked her head through the door to remind them it was bedtime, the incident had developed into a full-fledged curler war.

The following morning, Kerrie got up early to give her new hairstyle a quick touch-up with the curling iron, then spent the next half hour figuring out what to wear. She finally settled on her cream-colored prairie skirt, her brown cowboy boots, and her new rust blouse that had a flattering scoop neckline. She added some eye makeup and a touch of lipstick, then stood back to study the completed effect.

It came to her as somewhat of a surprise that she actually *was* pretty.

Not until it was time to go did she remember about her homework, which had somehow slipped her mind the night before. She felt a tiny stab of guilt, which evaporated the moment she walked into the kitchen and her dad looked up from his paper and whistled.

"I've got to hand it to you girls. When you decide to grow up, you sure do it in a hurry. You look absolutely gorgeous, Kerrie. What's the occasion?"

"Oh, nothing special," she lied. She sat down at the table and poured herself a bowl of granola. "Where's the sugar?"

"It's sweet enough without anything. Try it," her mother said. "Sugar rots the teeth. I'm trying to cut down on dental bills."

Kerrie sighed. "Where's Les?"

"Upstairs." Mr. Stewart winked. "Undergoing a beauty treatment, I suspect. I said Robbie could pick her up for school. He seems like a nice boy."

"Nice *young man*," Mrs. Stewart interrupted with a knowing look. "Like it or not, Ted, your daughters are growing up."

Kerrie's stomach was behaving strangely again; after a few bites of granola, she suddenly didn't want any more. She pushed her bowl aside.

Mrs. Stewart looked up from the stove, where she was frying a panful of eggs. "Are you feeling all right, Kerrie? You look a little flushed. Come here, and let me feel your forehead."

"I feel fine, Mom," Kerrie protested, a little annoyed that her mother could think of her as grown-up one minute and as a little kid the next. "Allison's picking me up—I've got to go, I'm late already."

She gave them both quick pecks on their cheeks and went flying out the door. Allison's Datsun came hurtling down the driveway not more than a minute later.

Allison's reaction was similar to what Kerrie's father's had been. "You look fantastic, Ker. What did you do to your hair?"

"Leslie did it. I have to let her take all the credit." She slid into the backseat to leave room for Jill in front.

Allison shook her head and adjusted her sunglasses against the early morning glare. "Some people have all the luck, I guess. First, a genie, now you've got a fairy godsister as well. What next? Is this where the prince rides up on his white horse?"

Kerrie giggled at the thought of Mike galloping up on a white horse. "I'm not sure I want to know what's next," she said.

*   *   *

On her way to homeroom, Kerrie ran into Mike coming out of the nurse's station down the hall.

"Checking up on me, huh?" he greeted her, displaying the aspirin tablet. "I hope you're satisfied. I told Miss Bruener I got hit in the head by a basketball, and she wanted to examine me for bruises!"

Kerrie walked down the hall with him. "And I thought that was going to be one of the easy ones. What else have you gotten so far?"

He reached into the pocket of his windbreaker and fished out a button that said NO NUKES in bold black letters. "That one was easy—Jamie Kline has the locker next to mine in gym. I just waited until he was in the shower, then I pinched it off his jacket. He's got so many others, he'll never miss it."

"We'll have to give it back to him when we're finished," she said. "I wouldn't want anyone to think we're doing this for profit."

Mike was staring at her, and Kerrie got so nervous she almost dropped her books.

"You look different," he observed. "Your hair. It looks nice."

"Thanks." She could feel herself blushing.

"You're really pretty, Kerrie—but you must have guys telling you that all the time."

She didn't know whether to say yes and

sound like a flirt, or no and have him think no one had ever complimented her.

She ended up smiling and not saying anything. Then she remembered what Allison had told her just as she was turning into her classroom.

"In case I forget to tell you later on, Mike, good luck with the game tonight."

He looked surprised at her interest. "You going?"

"I wasn't planning to, but—"

"You're not doing anything else, are you?"

"Well, no."

"Why don't you come then? Maybe we could go out afterward and get a bite to eat or something."

Kerrie was sure her answer was written all over her face. It was hard to sound casual as she said, "Sure, Mike, I'd like to."

"Great! By the way," he added, giving her a mysterious wink, "meet me out in front at lunchtime. I have a surprise for you."

Kerrie floated through the rest of the morning, wondering what it could possibly be.

"What's the first thing most people would wish for if they had a real genie?" Mike asked, cradling a shoebox under one arm as they strolled across the lawn at noon.

"Gee, Mike, I don't know." Kerrie frowned in concentration. "To be rich, I guess."

"What else?" With a flourish, he whipped the lid off the box. "Madam, I now pronounce you a millionaire. Or is it millionairess?"

Kerrie stared at the money stacked inside the box, then began to laugh. It wasn't really money, of course, but what Mike had done with green paper and a printing press was pretty good.

"I got to thinking last night," he explained, "and I remembered those caricatures we did of each other at the beginning of the year. I still had the one I did of you, so—a little print-shop magic and *presto*." Kerrie took a closer look, and sure enough, on each "dollar" bill was a tiny caricature of herself and printed underneath: "Kerrie Kurrency—in commemoration of Junior Genie Week, 1982."

"I can't believe it" was all she could say, unable to stop grinning.

Several people stopped to admire Mike's handiwork, and soon they had succeeded in attracting a small crowd. Mike and Kerrie handed out a few of the bills as souvenirs, and then Kerrie turned to whisper something in Mike's ear. He scurried off to fetch some string, a hole punch, and scissors, and a few minutes later they were busy looping strings of the funny green bills over the branches of a sycamore sapling planted a few feet away.

"Who says money doesn't grow on trees?" yelled Mike for the benefit of the onlookers.

Jill and Allison joined the crowd, shouting to Kerrie and grinning. A slight breeze scooped up some of the loose bills and sent them skittering across the grass, and a number of kids followed in hot pursuit. It was turning out to be one of the most imaginative stunts of the week. Bill Glass, photographer for the *Glenwood World*, even took a picture of the money tree when it was finished.

"I cast my vote for you two," he commented, snapping shut his leather camera case. "I like a couple with style."

Kerrie and Mike beamed at one another.

Later, Allison whispered to Kerrie, "Did you catch the look on Marcy's face when she walked by a few minutes ago? It's a good thing murder isn't legal, that's all I can say."

Nothing can touch me right now, thought Kerrie happily. *Not even Marcy.*

Chapter Eleven

The gym was ablaze with lights when Kerrie and Allison arrived shortly before eight o'clock. The bleachers were filling up rapidly with noisy crowds—Glenwood was playing Atherton, Allison informed her, and the two teams were tied so far for the season; so it promised to be an exciting game.

Kevin's sister, Meredith, had saved them seats in the front row. Kerrie caught sight of Les and Robbie as she was sitting down, and she waved furiously to get their attention.

"Hi, Al. Hi, Kerrie," Meredith greeted them, flipping her long strawberry blond hair over her shoulder. "Gosh, I thought you'd never get here. The game's going to start any minute!"

The starting five came trotting out into the

center of the court. Allison picked out Kevin at once—which wasn't hard, since he was so tall. She yelled at him, waving wildly. He broke into a grin when he saw her and waved back. Mike was right behind him.

"Mike's left guard," Allison whispered to Kerrie.

Kerrie nodded. "Oh." She wasn't positive what that meant; she was more impressed with how tanned and muscular Mike looked in his orange-and-white jersey. His eyes scanned the bleachers and finally met hers. He waved, and she gave him the thumbs-up sign, smiling broadly.

Unexpectedly, the crowd broke into raucous cheering and whistling as gangly Skeeter Hollis dribbled the ball out onto the court, dressed in his moth-eaten dress. His gigantic feet became tangled in the hem, causing him to trip, which nearly brought down the house.

Bringing up the rear was Tom Gates in a wheelchair, being pushed by his genie, Sparkey Knowles. Tom's leg was in a cast—he'd broken his ankle the week before—so he wouldn't be playing in the game, but it was apparent he was determined to share in some of the glory. Skeeter tossed him the ball, and Tom managed to dribble it over to the basket with a little help from Sparkey. He took aim from his chair and shot, scoring. Cheers from both sides erupted, accompanied by stamping feet.

The referee's whistle blew, and the game began in earnest. Kerrie didn't understand most of what was going on, except when Allison stopped screaming long enough to tell her.

". . . unbelievable, what a drive shot!"

". . . Mike's got that forward blocked so they can steal the ball."

". . . Kevin just scored a long jump shot. Two more for us!"

By the end of the first quarter, the scoreboard showed: Glenwood—12; Atherton—15.

With a twirling of their orange-and-white skirts, the pom-pom girls took over the court. Kerrie couldn't help noticing how Marcy stood out from the other four girls, especially when she did high kicks. Was Mike noticing it, too?

"I can't believe what a show-off she is," muttered Allison. "But I have to give her credit, she *is* good. And she knows it."

The girls formed a circle with Marcy in the middle. As they fanned out, doing their kicks, Marcy leaped up in a midair split, then spun immediately into a perfect cartwheel. The crowd applauded wildly, and there were several ear-splitting whistles for the way Marcy looked in her short skirt.

Mike, Kerrie saw, was standing over by the bench, huddled in conference with the coach. Boldly, Marcy trotted over to whisper something in his ear. Mike grinned and said something back, which made Marcy laugh. Watching them together, Kerrie felt sick. How could she be sure of Mike one minute, and so unsure the next? Was it true that Mike just liked to flirt? And was that all he had been doing with her all this time? Maybe she'd never been in competition with Marcy at all. Looking at Marcy, Kerrie thought Mike was totally out of her league.

Allison, noticing her discomfort, tried to distract her. "I hear that new pizza place they opened up downtown is really good. They even have live music. Kevin and I thought we'd try it out after the game. Do you and Mike want to come along?"

"I don't know," said Kerrie. "I'll have to see what Mike wants to do. Maybe he won't feel like going anywhere after all."

Allison gave her a funny look. "What's wrong, Ker? You don't sound very enthusiastic."

"Sure I am. I just have to talk to Mike first."

She would have given anything to have him walk over and talk to her. But he was still deep in conversation with Marcy. Kerrie couldn't take her eyes off them, even though it was torture to see them together. She told herself she was nuts to have ever thought Mike could care for her the way he obviously cared for Marcy. Holding hands was no big deal—friends did it all the time. Why had *she* made such a big deal out of it?

Then the whistle blew, and once again she was caught up in the confusing excitement of the game. The screams and yells around her were deafening. By the fourth quarter, the two teams were tied, and the game went into overtime. Allison had been shouting so hard, her voice was reduced to a hoarse croak.

In the last seconds, Gordon Hastings, Glenwood's team center, dribbled the ball to Kevin, while Mike blocked an Atherton forward. Then the ball was in Kevin's capable hands, and he moved into position for an outside shot. There was a blur of hands as the ball went streaking toward the net to bounce down squarely against the rim. It balanced there for a breathtaking instant, then slowly rolled in. The scoreboard lit up in Glenwood's favor, and the crowd exploded.

"See what you've been missing all this

time?" Allison told her, jumping up and down in her seat instead of screaming. Then she saw Kevin's head bobbing toward her, and she disappeared into the confusion on the court.

Where was Mike? Kerrie stood up on the bleachers to try to catch a glimpse of him, but he'd apparently been swallowed up by the postgame hysteria.

"Looking for someone?" a sarcastic voice asked.

She looked down and saw Marcy standing before her, hands on hips, an angry scowl on her lovely face. Warily, Kerrie stepped down to face her.

"Actually, I was looking for Mike," she replied evenly, surprised by her boldness. "He promised to meet me after the game."

Marcy snorted as if she found the whole thing vaguely amusing. "You still don't get it, do you?"

"Get what?" In spite of herself, Kerrie was beginning to become angry.

"You still don't see that Mike is only being so nice to you because he *has* to. You don't know him as well as I do, or you'd realize that. He's too sweet to want to hurt anyone's feelings, so that's why I'm telling you now—

because I can see you're going to be even more hurt when you find out the truth."

Kerrie felt as if she'd been hit in the stomach, but she had too much pride to let Marcy see that.

"Thanks for your concern, Marcy," she managed coldly. "But I can take care of myself."

Marcy's mouth narrowed to a thin line. "You really think so? Well . . . I guess we'll see about that, won't we? By next week when all this genie nonsense is over with, we'll see about a lot of things."

"I don't know what you're talking about."

"Oh, I think you do. God knows you're smart enough to figure it out, Kerrie." She stuck her face close to Kerrie's. "Just remember one thing, though—it's *me* he's taking to the dance on Saturday, not you. In case you might have forgotten."

Just at that moment, Laura Patterson showed up. She cut Kerrie with an icy look. "What are you wasting your time with her for, Marcy? Come on, let's get going, or we'll be late. The guys are waiting for us outside."

"Let's go then," she said, turning to her friend, her bright smile once again fixed in place. "This conversation is a dead end anyway."

Kerrie fought her way outside through a

blur of tears. Her face was burning, but the rest of her felt cold and numb. She didn't even feel Allison grabbing her arm.

"Hey, Kerrie, what's the big rush? Slow down . . . I'll be with you in just a sec. Kevin's talking to Mike about—" She stopped when she saw the look on Kerrie's face. "Hey, what's the matter, you look like you just got hit by a truck."

Not quite . . . but close. "I—I don't feel very good, Al. My stomach—"

"Uh-oh. Too much excitement, huh? I should have remembered this was your first time and not yelled in your ear so much. Come on, I'll take you home."

"No, it's OK, you go ahead. I'll get a ride with Les and Robbie. I see them over there."

Allison hesitated. "Don't you want to talk to Mike first?"

"No!" Kerrie almost shouted. Then she added more evenly, "Just tell him I went home, OK?"

"Sure. Take it easy, Ker. Hope you feel better."

Kerrie nodded and hurried off, wondering if she should have told Allison the truth. Except that she really did feel sick. She felt weak all over, and her knees were trembling.

Kerrie thought that the real reason she didn't tell Allison was that she knew what

Allison would say. Allison would have laughed off the whole thing and told her Marcy was jealous. Well, maybe that was partly true, but Kerrie couldn't forget the terrible impact of her words. Because she knew, deep down, that Marcy was right. Everything she'd said was only an echo of Kerrie's worst fears.

She stumbled into the fresh air, gulping in deep breaths, trying to hold back her tears. All she wanted was to go home, close the door to her room, and be alone.

The phone was ringing down the hall.

Kerrie had just put her pajamas on and was climbing into bed, when Mrs. Stewart knocked on her door.

"Come in," she called weakly.

"That was Mike," her mother told her. "He wanted to know how you were feeling, but I told him you were in bed, so he just left a message. He said to tell you that he has everything on the list, and he'll be picking you up for school tomorrow to go over it."

"Thanks, Mom. I didn't feel like talking to anyone."

Her mother came over and felt her forehead. "I *thought* you looked a little flushed this morning."

"Guess I have a touch of the flu or something."

"I think you should stay home tomorrow then."

Kerrie looked horrified. "I can't do that, Mom! Tomorrow's the parade. Mike's counting on me!" Whatever feelings she had about him right now, she couldn't let them affect their plans.

"Well . . . let's see how you feel in the morning. By the way, how was the game? You disappeared into your room so fast, I didn't get a chance to ask you. I gather from Les it was pretty exciting."

"Yeah, I guess so. I don't know much about basketball."

"I'm glad you're learning then. You know, Kerrie, I've thought a lot about what you said the other day. Maybe you were right not wanting to put *so* much emphasis on your studies. I do think it's important, and I know you do, too, but these last few days . . ." She smiled. "Well, I'm just glad to see you enjoying yourself so much. I guess I'd forgotten just how much fun it is to be sixteen. You're only young once, and it's not wrong to take advantage of it. As long as you keep things in perspective."

Her mother's words seemed to hang in the air after she left. *As long as you keep things in perspective.* Isn't that just what Marcy had been telling her in so many words? Next week, it would be different, she'd said. . . .

Kerrie switched off the lamp on her nightstand, thinking of the lamp in the museum and suddenly feeling foolish for the way she had acted that day—pretending there was magic, when all along it was just her imagination.

Chapter Twelve

Kerrie eyed the poster propped up in the backseat of Mike's VW. He'd covered it with a piece of newspaper. "Can't I at least take a peek?"

"I'll show you when we get to school," he told her as he drove. "I want to check out the expression on your face when you see it."

"I'm sorry you had to do all the work yourself, Mike, I should have—"

"Forget it," he cut her off with a wave of his hand. "I needed the experience. Thinking up all those captions was a little like coming up with advertising slogans."

"Did you really get everything on the list?" she asked.

"Not quite." One corner of his mouth curled up. "I had a little trouble getting Susie Epstein to part with one of her false eyelashes. She wanted to know what I was borrowing it for, so I told her I needed a fake spider to play a joke on my little brother."

Kerrie laughed. "More like a tarantula!"

In spite of the previous night's bitter experience, Kerrie found herself relaxing with Mike. He was so easy to talk to. He even laughed at her jokes. She was a little bit ashamed of herself for running out the way she had.

"And Miss Levenson caught me red-handed in her jelly-bean jar," he went on. "The way she acts, you'd think they were sacred or something."

Miss Levenson, the teacher for US government, had kept a jar of red, white, and blue jelly beans on her desk since the last presidential election. It hadn't taken long for everyone to figure out they were strictly for show—not to be eaten.

"Maybe you would have had better luck with the hundred-year-old kind," Kerrie suggested.

"Petrified jelly beans? No, thanks!"

Mike turned the VW into the school parking lot. He found a space and switched off the engine but didn't get out of the car right away.

"You know," he said, turning to face Kerrie, "I was really disappointed you had to leave so early last night. But when Allison told me you were sick, I got a little worried. You're OK now, aren't you?"

"I'm fine. I don't know what was wrong with me last night, it must have been something I ate."

"I was afraid you'd have to miss the parade."

"Are you kidding? I wouldn't have missed it for anything. You would have had to carry me around on a stretcher if I was really sick!"

"Now that's one trick I haven't quite mastered." He reached over the seat to pull off the newspaper covering the poster. "Ready for the unveiling?"

"I'm holding my breath!"

Kerrie marveled at the expert job he'd done mounting the items. And she couldn't stop laughing as she read the captions he'd typed up to go under each one.

Under a squashed-looking piece of fudge wrapped in plastic—one of the items on the scavenger list was "a failed recipe from Mrs. Boyle's home ec class"—was the caption:

BOYLE'S FAMOUS FUDGE—
GUARANTEED TO CURE ALL AILMENTS,
GROW HAIR, AND REMOVE WARTS!
(Money back if it doesn't kill you!)

There was the strand of Jaynie Cox's hair, and underneath it:

$$X + \text{JAYNIE COX} = \text{THE PALE ROOT OF A}$$
$$\text{NATURAL BLOND}$$

(See for yourselves, ye unbelievers!)

Skeeter Hollis's enormous battle-scarred sneaker dangled from the bottom with a funny tag stuck to the heel:

MULTIPLE CHOICE QUIZ:
Attached item is:
a) a dead animal of unknown species
b) a very small canoe
c) shoe belonging to Skeeter Hollis, Big Foot's city cousin
d) all of the above

"Mike, I didn't know you were so talented!" Kerrie complimented him, wiping tears of laughter from her eyes. "These are fantastic!"

He flushed with pride. "I can't take all the credit. It was your idea, remember?"

"But you must have stayed up all night doing these!"

"Not quite, but close," he admitted. "Anyway, I had a little help from Mom and Kurt. It was fun. Kinda like playing Scrabble."

"Well, I know I couldn't have done nearly as good a job myself."

"What . . . a genius like you?"

Kerrie wished he wouldn't keep telling her how smart she was—it made her uncomfortable. But she didn't say anything that might spoil the mood.

After a short discussion, they decided to put the poster on public display by the office, where it would get plenty of exposure before the parade. No sooner had they tacked it up than a group of kids began gathering, reading the captions aloud to one another. In a few minutes, everyone was breaking up, and the crowd got bigger.

Kerrie and Mike stood back, beaming at each other, totally satisfied. They had done it—as a team! She thought that whatever happened she'd never forget Genie Week.

The whole school turned out for the lunchtime parade on the football field. It was a warm, sunny day—perfect for the flimsy costumes a lot of the genies were wearing. Marcy turned up in her purple chiffon pajamas with an adoring Jeff Crosse in tow. Kelly Wiseman wore a shimmering sleeveless jumpsuit and a matching turban for the occasion.

The band started playing a sprightly version of *Scheherazade* while Linda Jordan in her donkey ears and a flowing print caftan kicked off the parade pulling Dave Palmer's now-famous wagon. Dave had sprayed a bunch of cardboard rounds with silver paint to make them look like coins and was tossing them to the onlookers as if they were all his adoring fans. To top things off, he was dressed in a sheet gathered to resemble a Roman toga. Judging from the applause and cheering, he was already a favorite for one of the prizes.

"The judges are going to love that one," murmured Mike to Kerrie. Between the two of them, they carried the poster that was already a legend at Glenwood. They wore their lady-and-the-unicorn costumes, which didn't hurt either as far as applause was concerned.

Several members of the Student Council and four teachers, including Mrs. Johannsen and Mr. Brandon, were judging the event. It was apparent that even the Duke could enjoy a good joke. A faint smile turned up the corners of his usually grim mouth as Greg Linville, his chin lathered with shaving cream, paused for Mark Reese to "shave" him with the ax he was carrying.

As everyone anticipated, it was Skeeter Hollis who stole the show when he pranced out and hiked the hem of his dress up to reveal a huge, floppy pair of rubber chicken feet. On his head he wore a rhinestone tiara, and he was carrying a bouquet of wilted dandelions. The crowd roared, giving him a standing ovation.

The PA system crackled. It was time for the judges to announce the winners. Mike gave Kerrie's hand an encouraging squeeze.

"Even if we don't win anything," he told her, "it's sure been fun . . . partner."

Kerrie didn't care if they won anything, either. Just being here, sharing the limelight with Mike and knowing she was accepted as one of his friends, made her feel as if she'd won something more important than any prize.

"Most Beautiful Costume is awarded to— Marcy Connaway!" Mr. Brandon announced crisply.

With a shriek of delight, Marcy skipped over to accept her prize of a gift certificate for one record album at the Turntable in Redwood City. The crowd applauded, giving her the usual share of whistles. Jeff Crosse looked as proud as if he'd won the prize himself.

To no one's surprise, Most Humorous Costume went to Skeeter, who made the most of his acceptance by flapping his elbows and running around in circles squawking. There were also prizes for: Best Teamwork—Linda Jordan and Dave Palmer; and Funniest Single Stunt, as voted by the entire junior class— Randy Cooke, the swimming pool fisherman. Then, in his dry voice, Mr. Brandon announced the last award.

"To Kerrie Stewart and Mike Price goes the award for Best All-Around Couple for their very individual stunts and the display of a unique scavenger hunt."

Mike grabbed Kerrie, lifting her off her feet and swinging her in a circle. "Didn't I tell you we were the best?" he yelled.

She was glad he was holding her hand when they went up to get their prizes—two gift certificates for albums—because otherwise, she felt she might have floated away. It was the best birthday present she could have imagined.

Afterward, Jill and Allison dashed over to congratulate her.

"It really *was* like something out of a book!" Jill screamed. "Now do you believe in happy endings?"

"Did you see the look on Marcy's face when you went up to get the prize?" Allison said. "I don't think she likes sharing the spotlight with you—or anything else, for that matter," she added slyly.

Jim Schumaker ambled by as they were talking. "Congratulations, Kerrie!" he called. "That was some display."

"Thanks," she said. "But Mike did all the work."

"That's what I like," he teased, "a girl who knows her place."

"Now just a minute . . ."

He grinned. "Just kidding. Price lucked out having you for a partner, that's all." He looked as though he wanted to say something more but changed his mind. "See ya around, Kerrie."

"Bye, Jim."

As they headed back to the classrooms Jill and Allison descended on her with questions about Jim. How did she know him? Was he going to ask her out? Would she go if he did? Kerrie could imagine how an overnight celebrity might feel, besieged by reporters.

It was like that for the rest of the day. People she hardly knew stopped her in the halls to congratulate her and say how much they liked the poster display. She saw Ron Kemp walking with his arm draped about Sylvia Hendricks's shoulders.

"Nice going, Kerrie," he yelled, holding up

his fingers in the OK sign. "I always knew you were a winner!"

Not even the low score she got back on Tuesday's Spanish quiz could bring her down. At the bottom of the mimeographed sheet, Mr. Garcia had scribbled in red pen: "What happened, Señorita Stewart? I hope it's just this week's craziness and nothing permanent. Study harder next time!"

How could anyone think of studying during Genie Week? she asked herself. She was still confused and uncertain about Mike, but she knew one thing for sure—things *were* different for her than they'd been a week ago. People noticed her. Boys acted interested. She wasn't just plain old Kerrie the Brain anymore. Even if she didn't get to be Mike's girl, she was definitely *somebody* at Glenwood High.

Chapter Thirteen

Kerrie sampled the guacamole dip with her finger.

"You don't think it's too salty, do you?" she asked her mother, who was standing at the counter cutting up celery stalks. "Too much onion?"

The lasagne was bubbling in the oven, sending a delicious smell throughout the spacious, Spanish-tiled kitchen.

Mrs. Stewart smiled. She had changed from her old gardening clothes into a becoming yellow and white print dress, which showed off both her dark tan and slender figure.

"I think if you keep hovering over that dip you're going to be too full to eat any dinner," she said. "It's fine! Mike will love it, so quit worrying and relax."

How does a person quit worrying about her first real date with the boy of her dreams? Kerrie wondered. Of course, she knew it wasn't *exactly* a date, but she was hoping Mike would want to take her somewhere afterward. Especially when he found out it was her birthday. Enough time had elapsed since Marcy's cruel warnings, and Kerrie was beginning to let herself hope again.

She was jolted from her thoughts by Leslie's sudden appearance in the kitchen. Les grabbed a stalk of celery from the cutting board and made a dive for the guacamole, managing to get away with a substantial glob before Kerrie snapped her away with a dishcloth.

"Next time I'll really get you!" she called to her sister's retreating back.

"Then I'll tell Mike that you've got his name scribbled all over the inside of your looseleaf!" she threatened mischievously.

"If you dare . . ."

Mrs. Stewart sighed and shook her head. "Girls!"

At a quarter to six, Kerrie took a shower and put on the new outfit her parents had given her for her birthday. Carefully she applied makeup and combed out her hair. When she finally stood back to examine the finished results in the mirror, she was pleased by what she saw.

The full skirt was a beautiful pastel blue with matching vest; the blouse a dark green paisley with long sleeves and tiny buttons along the cuffs. "Classic," was how her dad had described it. Yes, that was exactly right. For the first time, she really felt a year older, and she even tore the cellophane off a brand-new pair of panty hose for the occasion.

At six-thirty sharp, the doorbell rang announcing Mike's arrival. Kerrie was so jittery that she dropped her hairbrush twice, then nearly tripped on the telephone cord as she was on her way out to meet him.

Mike was talking animatedly to her parents when she got to the living room. His eyes lit up when he saw her. "Hey, Kerrie, you look great! What's the occasion? I thought this was going to be an ordinary dinner, but you look like you're expecting a VIP."

"Actually, Mike, it's my birthday," she confessed, a little chagrined by the fact.

Mike looked uncomfortable all of a sudden. "Why didn't you tell me? I feel like such a jerk. If I'd known, I never would have brought over all this stuff." He indicated a pile of books on the coffee table. "You see, I have this English paper to write over the weekend, and I sort of thought since you offered, you wouldn't mind helping me get a start. If I'd known it was your birthday . . ."

There was an odd stiffness in Kerrie's face when she answered after an embarrassingly long silence. "It's not your fault, Mike. You're right, I should have said something. I just didn't think it was all that important."

Before it had really begun, the evening was ruined for her. And it was all her own fault. What had made her think Mike would consider her invitation anything but an ordinary one to have dinner at a friend's house? She had kidded herself into thinking of it as a date, while Mike was behaving exactly as she might have if she were going over to Jill's or Allison's. He had brought his books over so she could help him with his homework. Kerrie the Brain—those words came back to taunt her. *Hello everybody, I'd like you to meet my good friend, and straight-A student, Kerrie Stewart.*

Kerrie had never felt so miserable in her whole life. Dinner seemed to last forever. She could barely eat, much less keep up her end of the conversation. She could sense Mike's discomfort, too, and once or twice, he shot her a questioning look. But she couldn't meet his eyes.

Instead, she listened to Mike answering her

parents' polite questions about school and his family. Leslie chattered on about the basketball game, reminding Kerrie that she herself hadn't discussed it with Mike. How dull and one-sided she must seem in comparison to her lively sister!

Dutifully, she blew out the candles on her cake—all sixteen of them. But she didn't make a wish as she had in previous years. What was the use of wishing for something she could never have? Her ice cream melted in a sorry little pool on her plate, and she only managed a bite or two of her favorite banana cake. Mike, on the other hand, finished seconds of everything and gave them rave reviews. Clearly, he was more interested in the food than in her, Kerrie decided.

After dinner, Kerrie's mother discreetly disappeared into the kitchen, while her father went into the den to finish some paperwork he'd brought home. Leslie was already off somewhere on another planet, giggling on the phone with one of her friends about Robbie. Finally Kerrie and Mike were alone in the living room.

Mike cleared his throat while staring at a painting on the opposite wall—a watercolor of a stormy ocean her father had done.

"Your mom's a terrific cook," he said.

"I know."

"My mom's pretty good, too, when she has the time—which isn't very often."

"That's nice."

Another silence, then he tried again. "I'll bet your family was pretty excited when you told them about the parade."

"Yes."

"Did I tell you? Mr. Thomas wants to put the poster up in the office. Guess he figures it'll kind of liven it up. That OK with you?"

She shrugged. "It's your poster."

Mike was staring at her now, and his face was drawn. "OK, Kerrie, out with it," he demanded. "What's bugging you? You've been acting like you didn't want me here ever since I came. I'm sorry I didn't know it was your birthday . . . but you could have told me, you know."

"It's got nothing to do with my birthday!" Kerrie knew she was acting terribly childish, but she couldn't seem to help herself. "Look, Mike, it doesn't matter. Really. You don't have to be nice to me anymore."

Mike looked furious. "What's that remark supposed to mean? You think this whole week has been some kind of an act? I don't get you, Kerrie. I don't get you at all!"

"Oh, what difference does it make?" she

cut him off. "You don't have to be with me anymore, so what do you care what I think?"

She kept her clenched hands hidden beneath the folds of her skirt and swallowed hard to keep from crying.

Mike stood up. "You know, Kerrie . . . I really thought we were friends. Just goes to show how wrong a person can be."

Kerrie didn't say anything until he had started for the door. Then she called softly, "Don't forget your books, Mike."

He gathered them up from the table. "Tell your mom thanks. It was a great dinner."

Then he was gone, and she could hear his VW starting up noisily in the driveway. He'd never speak to her again, Kerrie thought, as she dissolved into tears.

Chapter Fourteen

Allison called the next morning while Kerrie was still in bed.

"You're going to the dance tonight," she informed Kerrie before Kerrie could even open her mouth to say hello.

"What on earth are you talking about? I hope this isn't your warped idea of a joke, Al."

"It's no joke," she said, rushing ahead recklessly. "You see, Kevin has this friend—you don't know him, his name's Brian, uh . . . Brian Smith. Anyway, he was going to the dance with this girl and—you're never going to believe this—last night they broke up!"

"I still don't see what that could possibly have to do with me."

"Wait a sec . . . you didn't let me finish."

She took a deep breath. "After Brian told Kevin and me about the break-up and all, well, Kev happened to mention about me having this really terrific friend—"

"Oh no, Al, you didn't!" Kerrie cried in horror.

"Relax. I didn't tell him you hadn't been asked. I made up this story about what a coincidence it was because your date had been canceled, too—something about his having to leave town suddenly on a family emergency. After all, I didn't want Brian to think you were desperate."

Kerrie moaned, fully awake by now. "How could anyone think that?"

"The terrific part, I mean this is really *terrific*, is that *he wants to take you*! I told him I was sure you would go, but I'd have to ask you first, of course."

"Oh, Allison, how could you? You'll just have to tell him I can't."

"Of course you can," she stated in a tone not unlike Kerrie's mother's when she wanted her to do something. "It's all arranged. You're going with Kev and me. Brian's meeting us at the dance, since he lives way over in Redwood City."

But Kerrie could be equally stubborn. "I'm not going. I have nothing to wear, for one thing. And for another, you know perfectly well how humiliating it is to be asked at the last minute."

"What could be more humiliating than staying home?" Allison wanted to know. "Besides, it's already arranged."

Kerrie sighed out loud. "Next thing you'll be telling me I'm like Cinderella because my sister's going and not me."

Allison giggled. "You said it. Speaking of Cinderella, we've got to do something about a dress for you. I've already called Jill, and we're picking you up in an hour to go shopping at the mall."

"Don't I get any say in this at all? After all, it is my life you seem to be planning. Suppose I would rather sit home." It didn't sound convincing, even to herself.

Allison paused before answering. "Honestly, Kerrie, sometimes you don't make any sense at all! I thought you were dying to go."

Yes, but with Mike. She winced at the memory of the fiasco the evening before. "But I don't even know this Brian. I've never even heard of him. What's he like?"

"I'll tell you all about him when I get there."

Kerrie still had her doubts when Allison arrived to pick her up at nine-thirty, but at least she'd had a chance to think it over. In some ways, the blind date seemed like a perfectly awful idea. She had no way of knowing if she would like this Brian Smith, or vice versa—what if he hated her? She couldn't bear the thought of taking any more chances. And the prospect of seeing Mike at the dance, with Marcy in his arms, was like rubbing salt into a fresh wound. Still . . .

She *would* feel like Cinderella if she stayed at home, standing on the sidelines watching Les get ready. And if she went to the dance, at least no one could accuse her of inventing the bit about the blind date. It would at least be partly true.

In the end, she decided she would go.

"I knew you'd come around," Allison said, flashing her a smug look as they circled the shopping mall looking for a place to park. "You won't be sorry, believe me."

"Seems like I've heard that one before," Kerrie muttered.

"I've met him," Jill told her dreamily. "He's just your type, Kerrie."

"What is my type?" Kerrie wasn't sure she knew anymore.

"Tall and gorgeous," was all Jill would say, but her smile hinted at more.

"Great." Kerrie slumped down in her seat. "I've always wanted a date with Rhett Butler."

Allison found a space in front of Macy's, and they decided to go in there first after Jill fell in love with a dress in the window that was "just perfect for Kerrie." When Kerrie tried it on, however, the result was worse than Skeeter Hollis's gown. But after trying on several more dresses, she found one that fit her perfectly and looked just right. It was snug around the bodice, with spaghetti straps that left her shoulders bare; it was made out of a clingy, rose-colored fabric that had a soft sheen to it.

"It's beautiful, Ker," Jill said as Kerrie twirled in front of the mirror. "Brian's going to love it."

Suddenly tears filled Kerrie's eyes. "I wish I were going with Mike!" she blurted out.

Jill and Allison exchanged looks.

"What exactly did happen between you two last night?" Allison asked softly. "You didn't go into too much detail."

"I blew it," she confessed miserably. "Mike just wanted to be friends . . . and now he won't even want to be that."

Jill gave her an impatient look. "How do you know for sure he just wanted to be friends?"

Kerrie described the previous night's disaster in detail. "If a boy really likes a girl, he doesn't show up for dinner at her house with an armful of books, does he?"

Allison, seated on the bench behind her, crossed her legs and gazed up at Kerrie critically. "Who says? Kev and I study together lots of times."

"That's different. You two have been dating a long time."

Allison grinned. "We still manage to get romantic once in a while."

"Maybe you just got your wires crossed," suggested Jill helpfully. "You did say you offered to help Mike with his homework."

"But not on my birthday!"

"You can't blame him for not knowing it was your birthday, Ker," Allison reminded her coolly, "so why not chalk it up to bad timing?"

Kerrie glared at them. "Hey, whose side are you guys on, anyway?"

"Yours . . . naturally," Allison said. "What do you think this is all about, anyway?"

"I'm not sure," Kerrie answered doubtfully. "But I *do* know one thing—every time you two do something to straighten my life out, it gets more tangled up than ever. If it hadn't been for your birthday surprise, I wouldn't be in this mess in the first place."

"I'm hungry," Jill announced abruptly. "Let's go get something to eat."

They had lunch at the Soup Bowl, a tiny soup-and-salad bar squeezed in between Hallmark's and See's Candies. After they'd finished their clam chowder and coleslaw, Jill eyed the big creamy blocks of fudge in the window next door. Allison and Kerrie quickly steered her past—she was on another one of her diets and had made them promise on the way over that they wouldn't let her do anything she'd regret later on.

They spent the rest of the afternoon trying on clothes and makeup in the other department stores and a few of the smaller boutiques. To go with the dress, Kerrie bought a lacy fringed shawl and a new lipstick—something called Midnight Madness. Allison tried on a dozen pairs of shoes before finding some to go with her dress. Then she spent a whole hour sifting through evening bags before coming to the conclusion they were all hideous. All three girls allowed themselves to get talked into buying a facial pack by an over-eager saleswoman, who claimed the secret formula was guaranteed to make anyone look ten years younger.

"All I need," Kerrie said, giggling, "is to look six years old tonight!"

She was glad, after all, that she'd come shopping with her friends. It had certainly lifted her spirits. Now she could sort out her thoughts about the night before and reason more clearly. She felt stupid and childish for the way she'd acted. How was Mike supposed to know how she felt about him? She'd just assumed too much, that was all. In spite of Marcy's warning, she had gotten her hopes up.

Thinking back over the past week, she realized Mike had done nothing to really encourage her. Sure, he'd held her hand . . . but lots of people held hands without thinking about it, and Mike was the friendly, outgoing type. He'd told her she was fun to be with, he'd even told her she was pretty—but those were just compliments, and she had simply made too much of them. All he had wanted was to be her friend, and she had even made a mess of that. Some friend! She'd practically kicked him out of her house.

Suddenly Kerrie realized she'd rather be Mike's friend than nothing at all and that she had to stop worrying so much about her serious image. People weren't just one thing or another, she told herself—they were mixtures. Just as she'd surprised everyone with her sense of humor, she'd been surprised by Mike's serious side as well.

Was it too late to make up with Mike . . . as his friend? There wouldn't be a chance to find that out before the dance, and if she saw him at the dance—just thinking about *that* made her get weak—he would be too busy with Marcy to talk to her. She decided she would try to explain and apologize Monday at school.

Meanwhile, there was the dance to worry about—and Brian Smith, tall, gorgeous, and mysterious.

Chapter Fifteen

"Where's my brush? Has anyone seen my hairbrush?"

Leslie charged around the room in her slip, half her hair still in curlers, the other half loose in a mass of blond ringlets.

"Relax, Les, it's only a dance," Kerrie told her calmly from her dressing table, capping the bottle of nail polish and blowing on her fingernails to make them dry faster.

Leslie halted in the middle of her frantic rummaging. "*Only* a dance!" she said in outrage. "You're talking about the most fabulous night of my life! Anyway, I don't know what you're so calm about, you don't even know what your date looks like. He could be a cross between Frankenstein and Wolf Man for all you know."

Kerrie shrugged. "I don't care what he looks like . . . as long as he's nice."

She was determined not to be influenced by anyone's looks or popularity again.

Mrs. Stewart breezed in with Leslie's dress billowing on its hanger. "Room service," she announced dryly. "I ironed it for you, so don't go sitting on it until absolutely necessary. Good thing Kerrie's is the no-iron kind, or I'd really have my hands full. No one would guess you girls have been getting ready all afternoon!"

"My hairbrush," Leslie moaned. "I'll never be ready in time!"

Mrs. Stewart sighed as she picked up the hairbrush, partially hidden under a pile of crumpled tissues. "Here it is."

Leslie pounced on it. "Where did you find it?"

"Right under your nose. Where else?"

Half an hour later, Leslie was still rushing around when the door bell chimed and Robbie made his appearance in a dark suit and tie, carrying a small white florist's box. Kerrie watched in amazement as her sister sailed to greet him—as if she'd been ready for hours.

Robbie's eyes lit up. "Wow, Leslie! You look super." He nervously handed her the boxed corsage. "I got white. I didn't know what color your dress was going to be, so I wanted to stay neutral."

Leslie nearly blinded him with her metallic smile. "Gardenias! My favorite!"

They stood by the fireplace while Mr. Stewart fumbled with his Instamatic before taking half a roll of pictures. Then they floated out through the door, Robbie holding Leslie's arm as if it might break.

"See you at the dance, Kerrie," she remembered to call out to her sister. "And good luck with you-know-who."

Allison and Kevin arrived shortly afterward to pick up Kerrie. Kevin, looking like a scarecrow in his dinner jacket with the padded shoulders, pursed his lips in a long, low whistle.

"Brian's a lucky guy," he said. "You'll knock him dead in that dress for sure."

Allison pretended to glare at him. "How come I don't knock *you* out?" she wanted to know.

Kerrie thought Allison looked stunning in a mid-calf dress that billowed in layers of transparent apricot-colored chiffon. Her dark hair had been brushed until it gleamed, and she had pinned a silk rose over one ear.

"I have a feeling you will," Kevin teased,

holding his arms up in front of his face as if to protect himself.

Kerrie examined herself once more in the hall mirror on the way out. She did feel like a different girl tonight in this dress—a beautiful girl. It clung to her in soft, shimmery folds, emphasizing her slender figure and small waist. She was wearing her new lipstick, and her hair was caught up on both sides with glittering combs so that it fell in soft curls around her ears. Her cheeks were slightly flushed, even though she had used very little blusher, giving her face an added radiance.

Her mother hugged her at the door. "I hope this boy appreciates what he's getting."

Kerrie hugged her back. She'd made up her mind she wasn't going to let her disappointment over Mike spoil the evening.

The gym had been transformed. Kerrie gazed about her, nearly blinded by the dazzle of glittering colored lights that shone on the dancing couples. Instead of crepe paper, the walls and ceiling were festooned with gold ribbon, some of it woven together to resemble cobwebs. Shiny silver paper decorated the walls and the refreshment table, beside which stood an open chest with bright costume jewelry spilling out. One whole wall was covered with candid photos taken throughout Genie Week by photographers for the *Glenwood World*. A group of people had gathered in front of it, reliving the week's zany highlights with occasional bursts of laughter.

Allison and Kevin had disappeared into the crowd on the dance floor in search of Brian, so Kerrie wandered over to look at the photo display. Maneuvering her way over, she spotted several couples she knew—Ron and Sylvia, Laura Patterson and Eric Berger, and Robbie and Les. Leslie looked as if she were floating. Kerrie didn't catch sight of Mike and Marcy, for which she was grateful.

She was peering at a snapshot of herself streaking down the hallway on Mike's shoulders—*how had they managed to catch that?* —when she felt a hand on her elbow.

"Nice shot, huh?" A familiar voice called her attention. "I always told you we made a good team."

"Mike!" Kerrie whirled about and found herself confronting him. "I—I didn't see you when I came in."

"Good. I wanted to catch you alone first, to see if you were still speaking to me."

Relief swept over her. "Oh, Mike . . ."

He held up a hand. "Wait. I've got first dibs

on apologies here. I feel like a jerk about what happened last night. After Allison told me—"

"Allison!" Kerrie cried. "What did she tell you?"

"Don't blame her. I called her up after I got home. I had to know if she had any clues about why you were so mad at me." He smiled. "Let's just say she had a hunch."

"One of these days I just may end up strangling her!" But it was hard for Kerrie to sound murderous in her present state of happiness.

Mike's expression grew serious. "Kerrie, I'm sorry about last night turning out to be such a mess. I guess I pretty much figured you already knew how I felt about you."

Kerrie couldn't believe what she was hearing. "I—I thought you just wanted to be friends!"

"*Good* friends," he corrected, emphasizing it by slipping his arm about her waist. "By the way, I've got something for you—a sort of late birthday present. It's out in the car. Come on . . ."

Suddenly Kerrie remembered her blind date.

"Mike, I can't! I'm supposed to be meeting someone." In the back of her mind, she wondered about Marcy, too.

"Brian Smith?" he asked.

"How did you know?"

"Easy. I'll introduce you. Kerrie Stewart, meet Brian Smith, alias Mike Price." He bowed with a flourish and kissed her hand, sending tingles of warmth up her arm.

"How? . ." Her mind was spinning so fast she couldn't fit the pieces together.

"It's a long story," Mike began, "but I'll try and make it short."

It seemed that the afternoon before Marcy had confronted him in a jealous rage about Kerrie, demanding to know how he really felt about her. When he had confessed the truth, she was so furious that she broke their date for the dance—telling him she'd let Jeff Crosse take her before she'd go with him.

"When I talked to Allison, she told me your date for the dance had been canceled, too. I wanted to ask you, but I figured you'd be too mad at me to say yes. The blind date was her idea—she said you loved surprises."

Kerrie shook her fist, but she was laughing. "Oooh, I'm really going to get her for this . . . I really am, this time!"

They walked outside together, and for the first time she noticed how handsome—even dignified—he looked in his powder blue jacket and tie. When they got to his car, he handed her a beautifully wrapped package.

"Happy birthday," he said, sounding almost shy. "Better late than never."

Kerrie folded back the layers of crinkly tissue paper to reveal a gleaming brass lamp—a replica of the antique they'd seen in the museum.

"It's perfect, Mike!" she cried. "I didn't know you believed in magic!"

"Everybody needs a little magic," he said softly, his arms encircling her as he bent to kiss her.

His lips were warm and gentle, filling her with a sense of closeness she had never before imagined—not even in her wildest fantasies about Mike. The spring night surrounded her with its magic—the sky glittered with its millions of stars; the sultry air was perfumed by the scent of freshly cut grass; the distant music trickled out from the auditorium. . . .

He kept his arm around her shoulders as they went back to the dance. Kerrie felt as if she were floating two feet off the ground. She wasn't aware of anyone but the two of them, still caught up in the magic of their kiss. Mike tightened his arm and whispered, "Look over there, isn't that—"

"Jeff Crosse!" Kerrie exclaimed. "With Libby White."

It was a slow number, and Jeff and Libby

were dancing with their arms wrapped tightly around one another, swaying almost imperceptibly to the beat of the music. It was apparent Marcy's plan had backfired, but Kerrie was so happy right now she couldn't even feel smug about it.

Mike led her onto the dance floor, cupping her chin as he tilted her head back to plant a soft kiss on her lips. "By the way, I've been meaning to ask you something—how did a brainy girl like you end up with a screwball like me for a boyfriend?"

Kerrie closed her eyes, letting the warmth of his embrace seep through her, all the way down to her toes. "You never know about some people. . . ."

You'll fall in love with all the Sweet Dream romances. Reading these stories, you'll be reminded of yourself or of someone you know. There's Jennie, the *California Girl*, who becomes an outsider when her family moves to Texas. And Cindy, the *Little Sister*, who's afraid that Christine, the oldest in the family, will steal her new boyfriend. Don't miss any of the Sweet Dreams romances.

☐	22683	**SECRET IDENTITY #22** Joanna Campbell	$1.95
☐	22840	**FALLING IN LOVE AGAIN #23** Barbara Conklin	$1.95
☐	22957	**THE TROUBLE WITH CHARLIE #24** Jaye Ellen	$1.95
☐	22543	**HER SECRET SELF #25** Rhondi Villot	$1.95
☐	24292	**IT MUST BE MAGIC #26** Marian Woodruff	$2.25
☐	22681	**TOO YOUNG FOR LOVE #27** Gailanne Maravel	$1.95
☐	23053	**TRUSTING HEARTS #28** Jocelyn Saal	$1.95
☐	24312	**NEVER LOVE A COWBOY #29** Jesse Dukore	$2.25
☐	24293	**LITTLE WHITE LIES #30** Lois I. Fisher	$2.25
☐	23189	**TOO CLOSE FOR COMFORT #31** Debra Spector	$1.95
☐	23190	**DAYDREAMER #32** Janet Quin-Harkin	$1.95
☐	23283	**DEAR AMANDA #33** Rosemary Vernon	$1.95
☐	23287	**COUNTRY GIRL #34** Melinda Pollowitz	$1.95
☐	23338	**FORBIDDEN LOVE #35** Marian Woodruff	$1.95
☐	23339	**SUMMER DREAMS #36** Barbara Conklin	$1.95
☐	23340	**PORTRAIT OF LOVE #37** Jeanette Noble	$1.95
☐	23341	**RUNNING MATES #38** Jocelyn Saal	$1.95
☐	23509	**FIRST LOVE #39** Debra Spector	$1.95
☐	24315	**SECRETS #40** Anna Aaron	$2.25
☐	23531	**THE TRUTH ABOUT ME AND BOBBY V. #41** Janetta Johns	$1.95
☐	23532	**THE PERFECT MATCH #42** Marian Woodruff	$1.95

Prices and availability subject to change without notice.

SPECIAL
MONEY SAVING
OFFER

Now you can have an up-to-date listing of Bantam's hundreds of titles plus take advantage of our unique and exciting bonus book offer. A special offer which gives you the opportunity to purchase a Bantam book for only 50¢. Here's how!

By ordering any five books at the regular price per order, you can also choose any other single book listed (up to a $4.95 value) for just 50¢. Some restrictions do apply, but for further details why not send for Bantam's listing of titles today!

Just send us your name and address plus 50¢ to defray the postage and handling costs.
